STUCK ON YOU
AND OTHER PRIME CUTS

JASPER BARK

Paperback Edition

Crystal Lake Publishing
www.CrystalLakePub.com

To Veronica, my long suffering wife,

I've been stuck on you for so long, you're never going to shake me off.

And to my daughters Freya and Ishara, this is as much as you're allowed to read of this book until you're a LOT older, or I'm dead!

TABLE OF CONTENTS

FOREWORD

PAT CADIGAN

I wasn't ready for Jasper Bark the first time I met him.

I had agreed to do be part of a group reading in a Waterstones book shop in central London. It was a book launch, under the aegis of This Is Horror. I didn't know about This Is Horror events—specifically, I didn't know they were hosted by a congenial wild-eyed madman named Jasper Bark, and I didn't know that Jasper Bark obviously had some mad professional skills in the area of performing. Many writers don't, and why should they? Writing's creativity calls for concentration, attention to detail, and the fortitude to continue working without immediate applause. A thousand people may buy your book in a week; if two of them send you fan mail, it's extraordinary (unless you're Stephen King and really, who is? Besides Stephen King, I mean).

But some writers have a streak of greasepaint in them, so to speak, and Jasper Bark is one of them. I enjoyed his flamboyant, somewhat over-the-top introduction to the evening, welcoming the audience to the reading and informing them—warning them—that "*This* is horror."

The book being launched was by Joseph D'Lacey and, as there were vampires involved, someone had made blood fudge—i.e., dark chocolate fudge with a generous amount of red food colouring. It looked great to me. Jasper, however, had a problem with it. Something about sugar. He took a bite and choked so badly that he had to retreat to the green room during Joseph's reading. I was worried. Back in the mid-1980s, I became someone's mother and those instincts have never gone away. I tiptoed over to the Green Room to look in on Jasper, afraid that he might be lying on the floor and turning blue, unable to call for help.

Fortunately, he wasn't alone, although he and the lady with him were both startled to see me. They were standing several feet apart and she put her hands behind her back quickly, but I didn't think any of that. I was mostly worried about Jasper. When he assured me he was fine, I tiptoed back to my seat to catch the rest of Joseph's reading. Jasper reappeared just as Joseph finished and sat down so he could begin the interview.

Only Jasper really didn't look very good at all. He looked sick, definitely not like he could actually interview someone. Worse, if memory serves, Jasper also tried another piece of fudge. It didn't go down well. In fact, it didn't go down at all—and suddenly Jasper was writhing on the carpet, apparently having convulsions. I jumped out of my seat, horrified, trying to remember first aid for seizures and wishing I hadn't turned my phone off so I could dial 999. Assuming I could even find my phone in my purse.

And then all at once, Jasper was back on his feet and he was attacking Joseph. My jaw dropped. Jasper's wild eyes were practically popping out of his head and he had his hands around Joseph's throat

11

while he made these crazy, animal-like noises. I remember wondering what kind of convulsions would cause a person to physically attack someone.

I didn't catch on until Jasper tried to bite him.

And even then, I didn't realise until I caught sight of my husband in the audience; he was laughing. So was everyone around him but really, my husband was the tip-off. He is a sweet, compassionate soul who does not laugh at people having convulsions. I had been had.

Jasper, meanwhile, had dragged Joseph away in vampiric frenzy. Stage blood had splashed on the poster for the event and I was still trying to get my head around the fact that someone would go to such incredible lengths to put on this kind of show at a book launch—at a reading in a bookshop. And, omg, I had almost ruined it when I had gone to the green room to check on him. I had walked in on him while he was having his 'sick' make-up applied, and nearly caught her with pancake and sponge in hand. That was why he and the lady with him had been so jumpy.

So there you have it—Jasper Bark *got* me. And I loved it—it was one of the best readings I've ever been to.

I always love it when people really get into their material in a big way, when they decide to go for broke. Which brings me to this collection of stories by the very same wild-eyed Jasper Bark.

Chances are he is nowhere nearby so you are in no danger of him pouncing on you and grabbing you by the neck. Can't say the same, however, for the stories.

The material here is horror and Jasper has really gotten into the material in a big way. He goes for broke. In fact, some of these stories redefine broke, and then go beyond it. A few of them you may not be

III

ready for. But that's all right because they're ready for you. All of them are ready for you. Jasper knows just how to *get* you.

So don't fasten your seatbelt—it won't soften the impact. Don't even try to brace yourself. Just go with it and if you're kinda haunted by some of the things you've found in here . . . well, that's what you came for, isn't it? This is horror, Jasper Bark style. No one gets away unscathed.

Hell, they won't even let him back into Waterstones.

IV

STUCK ON YOU

CHAPTER 1

RICARDO CAME TO with the pain. He was lying on top of Consuela, his chin pressed into her naked shoulder. He lifted his head and blinked his eyes into focus.

Consuela didn't move. Her skin felt cold and clammy beneath his. Her eyes had rolled up into her sockets and her lips were drawn back.

Ricardo realized two things. The first being that she was dead. The second—that he still had his cock in her. He retched violently, his stomach heaved and he vomited all over her face.

It was getting dark, the ground they were lying on was damp. The still warm vomit was steaming in the evening air. It stank of stale beer and stomach bile. Ricardo gagged and tried to roll off Consuela.

A sudden searing pain in his stomach and loins prevented him. He cried out, trying to reposition himself so the pain would stop but it just kept building, shooting through him in growing waves. The agony became so great he couldn't even scream or sob anymore. He just gasped convulsively in silence until his body shut down and he passed out again.

CHAPTER 2

THE BLACKNESS BEGAN to fade. Ricardo felt as though he were resurfacing from a watery depth that no light ever reached. His mind struggled to make sense of the welter of sensations as he approached consciousness. It was like the moments just before waking when the dream you're having struggles to accommodate the sound of an alarm or another person stirring in your bed, building them into the scenario before the spell is broken and you open your eyes.

Ricardo felt a burning pain in his crotch and imagined that he'd penetrated a bonfire. The flames leapt higher as he thrust himself into the blazing mass. The pain and the flames were too intense. He didn't want to wake just yet, to face what they really meant. He wanted to hover just a little longer, unconscious, where they couldn't touch him.

As his waking mind became more aware of itself, Ricardo started to search for recent memories. What was happening to him? How did he come to be here? Why was he in so much pain? He needed to find the answers before he could wake and deal with the situation.

CHAPTER 3

THE FIRST THING Ricardo recalled was the blinding flash of light. There was a deafening crack that came with it. Like the sky had just shattered and the air around him had been torn apart.

There had been rain before that, light and refreshing. It relieved the humid air and made the night warm and moist like Consuela. She'd moaned and shaken beneath him like the thunder that crept up on them from afar.

They really should have listened to the thunder but it came up on them so quickly. Ricardo had been too distracted by Conseula, by her soft warm curves and the way they yielded to him. Then it had struck, as fast as lightning. No, it was lightning. They'd been struck by lightning.

CHAPTER 4

THE **SUDDEN MEMORY** jolted Ricardo awake. Without thinking he tried to sit up and instantly regretted it. He fell forward against Consuela and bit her shoulder with the pain. Her cool flesh tasted of his vomit.

Ricardo lifted his head with great care and turned to look over his shoulder at his butt. The skin around his coccyx was charred black and so swollen it had cracked and peeled. That was where the lightning had struck. It must have passed through him and into Consuela. She'd acted as his insulation. That's why he wasn't dead.

Ricardo placed his hands either side of Consuela's head and pushed himself up, as far as he could without hurting, so he could examine his body in the fading light.

The skin was missing from his most of his stomach and Consuela's. What little there was looked white and leathery. The rest of both their stomachs were nothing more than raw exposed tissue, red, wet and agonizingly sore. Across both their chests Ricardo could see curling burn marks, like blistering, red fronds, where the lightning must have discharged.

The shock of what had occurred was too great for him to take in at first. He'd been viewing the damage quite dispassionately, as though he wasn't in any way connected to it. As he looked down at the angry, suppurating wounds it began to sink in. This was his body. His once beautiful physique. He was scarred for life. He was never going to be the same.

Ricardo felt himself go cold and he retched again. Only bile came this time, burning the back of his throat. He began to cry. This wasn't fair. Why had this happened to him? Oh God it was so painful. He couldn't stop himself from shaking. His arms gave out and he fell forward onto Consuela's cool body.

More tears came at the random cruelty and unfairness of it all. He pressed his face against Consuela's bile soaked cheek and hugged her for comfort. Her body smelled rancid from the vomit with an underlying odor of burnt pork. His self-pity disappeared, melted by anger and revulsion.

He tried to pull himself out and roll off Consuela again. This time he was more careful but the pain was still unbearable. It wasn't just his raw flesh rubbing against hers, his cock felt like it was caught in a vice. Her muscles must have spasmed and seized up. They were clenched tighter than a fist. It must have happened when the lightning struck.

Adam, a med student friend of Ricardo's, once mentioned something about this. They were getting drunk and swapping horror stories. Penis captivus was the term Adam had used. He'd even shown Ricardo a YouTube video of some Kenyan guy who'd gotten stuck in another man's wife. The Kenyans put that down to some witchdoctor shit, not a lightning strike. Either way it was a rare occurrence. Probably as rare as getting struck by lightning while you were boning someone.

That made him think of something else he'd read online. An urban myth about a guy and a gal who were going at it on a hillside when they got struck by lightning. The rubber they were using melted and fused them together. Adam had said this would be impossible. The condom's latex would insulate his cock and even if it did melt it would just shrivel, there was no way it would stick to the gal's vaginal walls.

Yet here Ricardo was with his cock stuck in a dead woman. It wasn't right. The anger welled up inside him and he punched the ground. It wasn't enough. He needed to take his rage and frustration out on something else.

Ricardo looked down at Consuela with her up-turned eyeballs and bared teeth and he practically choked on his resentment. He reared up as far as he could and pounded his fist into her dead face. "Damn you," he shouted. "Damn you, damn you, damn you." He hit her twice more but the blows were ineffectual and she was so covered in vomit that his fist kept slipping off.

He heard a bone in her nose crack. Encouraged by the sound he hit her again, even harder, but the blow caused him to topple on to his side dragging her with him.

The physical torment this caused was beyond belief. His whole vision went white as the agony drowned out every other sense in his body. It was too much for him to remain conscious. The last thing that crossed his mind before he passed out was: "How the fuck am I going to explain this to Ellen?"

CHAPTER 5

IT WAS ALL Ellen's idea. She had this half-baked notion about setting up a stall at all the trade fairs and county shows around Arizona. It wasn't as though she needed the money. Her parents were richer than his. It was the romance of being an artisan trader that appealed to her.

So she'd sent him over the border to Nogales to cruise round all the curio shops they have downtown and buy up cheap 'artesanias'. This was the local name for the handicrafts they shipped in from Mexico's central and southern states.

Ellen said he had a better eye for this sort of thing than she did because it was part of his heritage, which irked him. His family had been in the States for three generations. Mickey D's, baseball and the Arizona Cardinals, that was his heritage.

Ellen thought that running a business venture would bring them closer together. It was more than that though, it was also a test. Sending him over the border was her way of seeing if she could trust him.

To be honest even Ricardo was surprised when she'd taken him back. They'd been dating since College and frankly he was bored. He'd started sleeping around behind her back, nothing too serious, just the odd casual lay here and there. He was discrete to begin with but he'd gotten careless over time. Maybe it was over confidence, or perhaps he wanted to get caught, he wasn't sure, but one stupid text message had sunk him.

Ellen had picked up his phone to order take out and spotted the text. Ricardo hadn't even slept with the girl but that was enough to arouse her suspicions. She scoured his cellphone, his tablet and his laptop. There was plenty of evidence to incriminate him.

She confronted him in the bath. Threw the phone at his head. Ricardo denied it of course but she had him bang to rights. She even quoted the Bible at him. Numbers 32:23: " . . . be sure your sin will find you out". Ellen's Sunday school Priest had told her that you carry your sins around with you and you can never shake them off. Catholic girls, they never let that sort of stuff go.

When he realized he couldn't bluff his way out of it he threw himself on her mercy and promised to change. He was almost relieved to be honest. He was never that great with secrets. They had a way of eating you up inside.

Ellen made a lot of stipulations and because he kept to a few of them she eventually relented. The sex got a lot better for a while and a lot more frequent. He guessed she wanted to reclaim him for herself and wipe away the taint of his other lovers.

It seemed like a new beginning for them and he didn't miss the other lovers at first. But in time things got a bit stale and that's when Ellen suggested running a stall. It was another of her grand gestures. She was big on those. Ricardo would scour Mexico for handicrafts, she'd sell them to bored hicks and they'd both reap the profits. At least, that's how it played out in Ellen's mind.

Handicrafts weren't Ricardo's first choice of import. If he'd had his way they would have traded something far cooler, like deadly species—tarantulas or flesh eating monitor lizards. Some of those things were so rare, or endangered, people would pay through the nose for them. Especially if there was a ban on selling or transporting them into the country.

Ellen was squeamish about that sort of thing though. She had her heart set on artesanias so Ricardo had jumped in his jeep and headed south.

He'd parked up just over the border in one of the Mexican lots. He couldn't stand driving in Mexico. There were no rules. Nobody stuck to their lanes or bothered with speed limits. They wove in and out of each other without any regard for safety, and the road signs bore so little relation to the turnings that they might as well be from another city.

The afternoon he'd spent wandering the little passageways off the main shopping area left him bored and resentful. He hated haggling with the dried up vendors who took one look at his clothes and his dental work and automatically trebled the price of everything. He rewarded himself with a tour of the titty bars and walked back to his car with a lazy hard on and a pleasant buzz from the cheap beer.

The beer they served in those joints was cold and gassy to hide the fact it tasted like shit. Ricardo belched hard as he strolled into the parking lot and tasted the burritos he'd wolfed down earlier. The locks on his Grand Cherokee clicked open as he approached, like a pair of open arms waiting to greet him. Keyless technology, you gotta love American engineering. The little card in his wallet meant his baby opened just for him. She was more loyal than any woman or dog.

She was better at hiding his secrets too. With lots of neat little compartments in the forward storage bin where he could stow his wares so customs wouldn't see 'em. He was so busy doing this he didn't notice Consuela till she spoke.

"Headed back to the states?"

Ricardo took his head out the trunk to look her up and down. His first impression was not flattering. She was quite short and passing pretty, with jet black hair and tanned skin. Her T-shirt was coming apart at one seam and her cut-off jeans were faded near to white with constant wear. She didn't have a great rack but her body was okay. She was most likely in her mid-twenties but she already had the beginnings of crow's feet around her eyes and lines about her mouth.

He took all this in as he regarded her. "Why do you ask?" he said, giving nothing away.

"Thought maybe you could give me a ride?" she said with a smile and more than a hint of suggestion.

"Why would I want to do that?" he replied.

"To help a gal in her hour of need."

"And what's in it for me?"

"Maybe you could use the company. It can get pretty lonesome on those long old roads."

"And how would you keep me from getting lonesome?"

"I might know a trick or two?"

"Listen, I'm not looking to pick up a hooker, so maybe you should try someone else."

The girl's eyes flashed at this. Her shoulders went

back and her chest rose with indignation. "A hooker? A hooker? Where do you get off calling me a hooker! Who do you think you are?"

Her sudden anger surprised Ricardo. He also found it exciting. He raised his hands by way of apology. "Look I'm sorry okay. I made a mistake. I thought that's why you asked me for a ride."

"I need to cross the border, that's why I asked you for a ride."

"What makes you think I'm headed back across the border?"

"You have a fancy American car. You don't have any suitcases and you're hiding things in your trunk."

Ricardo smiled. "Okay, you got me. But what about you? Why'd you need a ride so bad?"

"You ask a lot of questions."

"I'm just being careful. No offence, but I don't know you and I don't let just anyone inside my jeep. That's leather trimmed upholstery right there, you gotta show it some respect."

"And I don't get inside just anyone's jeep. If I choose to sit on your leather upholstery that's a sign of respect."

"It's leather trimmed and you didn't answer my question. Why'd you want a ride?"

Consuela patted her stomach. "I have something to deliver."

"You're pregnant?"

Consuela rolled her eyes at him, paused for a moment and pursed her lips as she considered her words. "There are things your government won't allow in your country, so people pay a lot of money for them. The people selling these things pay me a lot of money to get them there. If you give me a ride, with your leather trimmed upholstery and your US plates, customs won't bother me and I will be very grateful."

"How grateful?"

"You'll have to give me a ride to find out."

So that was it. She was a mule. Ricardo knew right then that he was going to give her a lift. The wise thing would be to turn her down flat. To get the hell out of that parking lot and not look back. But where was the fun in that?

Ricardo heard tales all the time about shoot outs on Mexican city streets. About the gangs who smuggled drugs and people over the borders. About how dangerous this lawless country was becoming. The truth was that he'd never seen so much as an argument on any of his numerous trips. He found the place dull and depressingly run down.

This was the first bit of excitement he'd ever encountered here. It also turned him on to think that he'd have power over the girl. She'd need to keep him sweet if he was her ride to Arizona. Ricardo walked around to the side of the car and opened the passenger door. "Hop in," he said.

As he climbed behind the wheel and headed back out onto the road Ricardo was palpably aware of her presence. The bare flesh of her shoulder, where her T-shirt had fallen, kept catching his eye. She crossed her legs and the denim rode up her thigh. The upholstery creaked in what sounded like appreciation as she shifted her weight.

Then there was her scent. It filled the cabin and hung in the air. Cheap soap and fresh sweat. Ricardo breathed it in as he drove. He closed the windows and turned down the climate control so he could enjoy it better. She caught him glancing over at her and smiled, savoring his attention.

"My name is Consuela," she said. "What is yours?"

"Miguel." He wasn't going to give her his real name. That would shift the balance of power in her favor. He didn't want her turning up later at his crib. A false name gave him distance from the situation, made it more of a game.

Ricardo pulled into one of the two lanes open at the border. The crossing was pretty quiet this time of day and there wasn't much traffic. He wound down his window as the customs official by the side of the road signaled for him to pull over. The man was tall and broad with a beer gut to match. He looked like he was used to intimidating people with his size. "Anything to declare?" he said checking their passports.

"Just a few souvenirs," Ricardo pointed to the leather art, hand-made flowers and Day of the Dead pottery he'd left in plain view on the back seat. The custom's official scanned it. "Anything worth more than $400?"

"Nope," Ricardo lied, he wasn't going to pay the tax. The customs official pointed to Consuela. "Is this lady in your employ, sir? A maid or something?" Ricardo didn't know what to say. He glanced at Consuela and saw the anger flash in her eyes again. "I am not a maid," she said leaning forward to look the customs official in the eye. She reached out and put her hand over Ricardo's crotch, grabbing his cock and balls. "This is my sex slave bitch!"

Ricardo sat bolt upright as Consuela's fingers closed around his groin. The customs official looked down at Consuela's hand. He could see Ricardo hardening beneath it. "Good luck with that one," he said and waved them on.

"Way to go not drawing any attention to us," Ricardo said.

"You know how many white guys want to be dominated by a hot Mexican tamale? I gave him a little fantasy to take home and jerk off to. You think he's going to spoil that by pulling us over." Consuela removed her hand as they drove off, but Ricardo remained hard for miles.

RICARDO CAME **R**OUND to the sound of snuffling and chewing. He was groggy, disoriented and wracked with pain. He didn't know where he was or why he was on his back.

His vision came slowly into focus. The snuffling noise got louder, punctuated by smacking lips. Ricardo smelled the hot, musky scent of a large animal and saw black fur.

There was a huge grizzly standing over him. No, it couldn't be a grizzly. There were no grizzlies in the forest, they were chased out centuries ago along with the wolves and the jaguars. It must be a black bear, but it was the biggest damn black bear Ricardo had ever seen. It had to be over 800 pounds and seven feet long. It could have taken his face off with one swipe of its paw.

The bear's muzzle was inches from his face. He could smell the animal's breath and see its huge teeth. It was licking the vomit from Consuela's face. It must have been attracted by the smell.

The huge beast shuffled closer and the claws of one paw grazed his shoulder. Ricardo winced with the pain. Consuela shook and the bear stopped licking her.

It lifted its muzzle and sniffed the air, checking for movement. Ricardo fought back his panic, drenched in sweat, his heart pounding.

His every instinct told him to flee but he was trapped beneath Consuela. Stuck inside her. He couldn't even stand, let alone run. Ricardo's only hope for survival was to lie as still as possible and hope the bear didn't notice him.

His blackened coccyx stung like crazy with the stones and the twigs digging into it, but he didn't dare shift his position or do anything to alleviate the pain. He couldn't risk drawing the bear's attention.

The bear's long pink tongue cleaned all the puke from one side of Consuela's face. It sniffed at her cheek, still hungry. The color was gone from Consuela's face but it must have looked good to the bear. It gave her cheek a few exploratory nips then drew back its lips and sunk its long yellow teeth into the side of her face.

Ricardo bit his own lip as the bear shook its muzzle and tore off a ragged chunk of flesh. A huge gobbet of blood and saliva dripped from its jaws and hit Ricardo in the face.

'Please, God, please let me black out again, please.' Ricardo's silent prayer went unanswered. All he could do was lie motionless beneath Consuela as the dirt of the forest floor dug into the blackened wound on his butt and the bear fed on his former lover.

He screwed his eyes shut and tried to block out the sound of the bear's jaws crunching through Consuela's cheek bone. He tried to disconnect himself from the situation. It had a strange familiarity about it. Like déjà vu or a story he'd heard before.

Then he remembered the urban myth. That had a bear in it too. Why was he living out some crummy campfire tale people told to gross each other out? Was that even possible?

He remembered a movie he saw once in a film studies class. Not one of the good ones with explosions and proper CGI effects, an old French movie with Orson Welles in it. The Immortal Story it was called. It was about a rich old creep who gets fixated on an urban legend about a sailor who's paid to knock up some old guy's trophy wife. He gets so obsessed with this story, that's told in ports all over the world, that he ends up employing some babe to pose as his wife and paying a real sailor to impregnate her. All because he wants the story to have actually happened, at least once, somewhere in the world.

Is that what was happening to Ricardo? Was this whole thing a set up to bring an urban myth to life? Or does every urban myth have to happen to someone, at least once, somewhere in the world? Ricardo cast his mind back to the events that led him here, in an attempt to find some answers.

CHAPTER 7

"**W**HERE YOU HEADED?" he asked as they pulled out onto the highway.

"The Coronado Forest," Consuela said. "Do you know it?"

"Sure, land of the Sky Islands, went hiking there as a kid. I can drop you off pretty near."

"Pretty near? You mean you're going to desert a gal in her hour of need? What kind of man are you?"

"A man with a schedule to keep."

"A man who's going to miss out on all the fun."

"Sorry, but I gave up hiking when I was a kid."

"Not my kind of hiking you didn't."

"And what kind of hiking is that?"

"As I said before, you'll have to give me a ride to find out."

She placed her hand on his knee and ran her fingers up the inside of his thigh. Her scent was stronger as she leaned into him, sharp and musky. Her fingers skirted the erection that was pressing against the top of his thigh. He felt the warmth from her palm and he throbbed against the tight denim of his jeans.

That was it. He was sold. He shot her a stupid grin and she knew she had him. She settled back into her seat and he ached with the sudden loss of her touch. The smell of her fresh sweat and cheap cosmetics hung in the air between them.

He lost interest in the traffic, snatching glances at her thighs and the faint outline of a nipple through her T-shirt. He started to imagine how she might look without any clothes. How her skin might feel against his. She saw him looking and pushed out her chest, inviting more attention, draping her arm over the back of the seat so that her fingers almost brushed his shoulder.

He began to run logistics. Ellen was expecting him that evening with the goods he'd bought. They were going to have dinner. He couldn't make it back from the forest before midnight. Might be risky driving some of the back-roads that time of night. Not to mention the people Consuela was going to meet. So long as he kept his nerve and his head down he should be fine though. Truth be told he was looking forward to the excitement.

He'd call Ellen later and feed her some line. Ricardo felt a sudden pang of guilt when he thought of Ellen. She could be a real pain in the butt sometimes but she'd been good to him. Maybe this wasn't a good idea after all.

Ricardo wondered how he might pull out of the deal now. He doubted Consuela would be easy to ditch. He remembered the customs official waving them through: "Good luck with that one."

Consuela reached up and stroked his cheek, tucking a strand of hair behind his ear, as if she sensed he was wavering. She stroked the back of his neck with her nails and sent static charges right across his shoulders. The follicles on the back of his neck tightened and his hair rose.

Perhaps he was allowed the odd indiscretion. So long as he was careful and didn't hurt Ellen by letting her find out. Ricardo didn't mind lying. It was secrets he couldn't take. They had a way of eating you up inside. He'd just have to keep these secrets deep inside him. Swallow them like the drugs Consuela had sitting in her stomach.

His thoughts were broken by a tinny text tone. Consuela pulled a disposable cellphone from her pocket and glanced at the screen. "Do you know the Mount Wrightson Wilderness off of Highway 19?" she said.

"Sure," Ricardo replied punching it into his sat nav. "Don't s'pose you got a zip code?"

Consuela shot him a wry look. "I don't know where the meet is yet. As we get closer they'll text me. That's how it works."

Ricardo was fascinated. This was totally outside his experience. The closer they got to 'the meet' the more his heart started to beat. He wasn't sure what excited him more, the promise of Consuela or his involvement in an illegal drugs deal. He was trying to play it cool but his curiosity was becoming hard to suppress.

"So how do you, y'know, deliver the stuff?" he said. "Do you have to drink castor oil or something? Do they give you a bowl?"

Consuela regarded him with amusement. She opened her mouth and reached in with her index finger. She hooked it under a thin piece of twine tied around her back tooth and lifted it for him to see. "I just pull it out," she told him.

"Was it hard to swallow?"

"No, I just relax and let it slip down. No different to deep throat."

Ricardo felt the sweat break on the back of his neck. Deep throat was the Holy Grail of sex for him. He'd never met a girl who could actually do it. A couple of his lovers had tried, but the results had been pretty ugly. Consuela saw his arousal and shot him a satisfied smile.

She got another text and directed him to the next turning. It was apparent that she'd done this many times before. It was unlikely that he was the first guy she'd taken up into the woods. That didn't bother him too much. It just meant there were no complications. They both understood what this was. He could get in and out without any problems.

The worst type of girls were the limpets. The ones who clung on afterwards and wouldn't let go. Who kept texting him saying they 'had to talk' then turned up at his crib unannounced. Consuela wasn't going to be anything like that. There'd be no problems separating from her afterwards.

CHAPTER 8

EVENTUALLY THEY PULLED up at the side of a dirt road near a wilderness trail. "What now?" Ricardo said. Consuela put her phone on the dashboard.

"Now we have to wait till they set a location."

"How long will that be?"

"I don't know yet, they've been held up. They're a couple of hours away."

"A couple of hours! I can't wait that long. I've got to be somewhere tonight."

"Oh come on, it's not all bad. I'm sure we can think of something to do to kill the time."

Ricardo let go of the steering wheel and turned to Consuela. A cold burst of anticipation filled his stomach. He saw the fine sheen of sweat on Consuela's chest. His breath quickened. Consuela raised an eyebrow, full of suggestion. He could hear his heart in his chest as he leaned in to kiss her.

Consuela placed her finger on his lips. It tasted of salt. "Not so fast," she said. "You don't think it's going to be that easy do you?"

"But I thought . . . you said . . . "

"Oh I say a lot of things."

Ricardo was confused. "What did I do wrong?"

Consuela opened the passenger door and slipped out. She sashayed into the trees.

"You didn't try hard enough," she called out over her shoulder. Ricardo frowned, staring after her as she went further into the forest. She turned for a moment and placed her hands on her hips. "Well what are you waiting for—an invitation?"

He smiled, understanding the game now, then jumped out of the car and went after her. Consuela began to run, darting in and out of the tall evergreens and laughing as Ricardo closed in on her. Twice he nearly had her, but each time she gave him the slip.

Finally he pressed her up against a tall oak, his hands either side of her shoulders to block her escape. "Thought you could get away from me huh?"

Consuela placed her hands on his chest. Ricardo was warm from running, but her palms were hotter.

"Thought you could catch me huh?" she countered.

He made to kiss her again and she tilted her head to evade him. She ran her hands down his chest and stomach, letting them settle on his crotch. He let out a quick breath as she cupped his balls with one hand while the other stroked his erection through the denim of his jeans.

Ricardo closed his eyes and pushed his crotch towards her, lost in the sensation of her fingers on his cock. This gave Consuela the perfect opening and she ducked under his arm and was off again into the forest before he realized what had happened. "Hey, no fair," he called and chased after her.

He followed Consuela to a clearing and then promptly lost her, as though she'd vanished into the scrub grass beyond the trees. He stood panting for a moment as he got his breath back. The sun was sinking behind the tops of the trees and heavy clouds were moving in.

A hand grabbed his shoulder and spun him round. It was Consuela. Ricardo lost his balance and she took advantage of this, pushing him up against a tree trunk. Before he could react she pressed herself against him and grabbed his neck, pulling him into a kiss.

Consuela's lips were soft and insistent. Her tongue darted in and out of his mouth stroking his tongue and stoking his need for her. His hands slid up and down her back as she tilted her pelvis and pushed her crotch against his.

He moved his lips to her neck, kissing his way down the soft flesh, pinching it with his lips and flicking out his tongue to taste the sheen of salt sweat on her skin. Consuela reached around, undid her bra and slipped off her top.

Ricardo slid his hands round to her front and cupped her breasts, small and firm against his palm. He brushed his thumb lightly over her dark brown nipples. She caught her breath and bit his shoulder. The sudden pain gave him a rush.

Ricardo kissed his way along her collarbone and down her chest. Consuela leaned back, pushing her breasts out as his lips circled her right nipple. He ran his tongue slowly round the tip, teasing it till it was firm and erect, then pressed it between his lips as Consuela groaned with appreciation.

The warm odor of her breast and the way the nipple hardened beneath his tongue set off a deep yearning in him. An appetite for her that seemed impossible to satisfy. It wasn't just the way she touched him and offered herself up to be touched. It was a deeper, more primal urge that made him want to melt into her and penetrate every molecule in her body.

Consuela wriggled out of her shorts and pants, then took hold of the hair on the back of his head and pulled him away from her breast. She bent his head back, put her other hand on his shoulder and pushed Ricardo to his knees with a strength that surprised him.

She placed her right foot on his shoulder and moved his head so that it was inches from her crotch. She was wet and he could smell her juices, hot and musky. "Do you want to taste me?"

"Oh God yes."

"Say please."

"What?"

She tugged at his hair making him wince. "Say please."

"Please."

She tugged again. "Say pretty please."

"Ow, pretty please."

"Good boy."

Consuela tilted her pelvis up and guided his head forward. Ricardo ran his tongue between her lips and up to her clitoris. She gasped as his tongue found the tender hood and the tight knot of flesh it hid. He circled them both with his tongue, slowly at first, building up a rhythm, keeping time with Consuela as she rocked her hips back and forth.

Ricardo could almost feel the pleasure burst from her clitoris, like ripples traveling a little further along her thighs and up her spine with each flick of his tongue. Consuela's moans became full throated cries as she rode the crest of an orgasm. Her fingers clenched into a fist in his hair. She pushed his face deep into her. Her juices spilled over his cheeks and dripped from his chin.

He couldn't believe how good she tasted, how hard he was. A huge shudder ran through her body as Ricardo's tongue increased its speed. Consuela let out a long, fierce cry of joy as the orgasm crashed through her and she ejaculated into his mouth.

The hot jet of liquid hit the back of his throat and he swallowed in surprise. His tongue darted back to her clitoris and she ejaculated again, crying out even louder as she filled his mouth. Ricardo swallowed and coughed as she let go of his hair and slumped against a tree to recover.

"Your turn," Consuela said as she straddled him and pushed him on to his back. She knelt over him, unbuckled his belt and pulled off his jeans and his boxers. His erection sprang bolt upright. Free at last. She took hold of him with her thumb and forefinger, encircling the almost imperceptible ring of sensitive tissue just below the base of his helmet. He stiffened in her hand as she gently rolled her thumb and forefinger up and down.

Tucking her hair behind her ear she bent over and put her mouth on his balls. The skin of his scrotum tightened as her tongue traced each ball and then moved upwards along the length of his shaft. As she got to the top Consuela rolled down his foreskin with her thumb and forefinger and brushed the exposed helmet with her lips.

His cock swelled and throbbed to the touch of her lips and he pushed himself closer to them. Ricardo lifted his buttock off the ground and Consuela withdrew just enough so that he could feel her breath on the end of his cock, but not her mouth.

"Say please."

"Not this again."

Consuela sat up and reached for the top she'd discarded.

Ricardo held out his hands. "Wait, wait, I'm sorry. Please, okay, pretty please with sugar and a million dollars and a big fat Cartier watch on top."

Consuela looked satisfied. "Now you're learning."

She took hold of his cock again and Ricardo doubted he'd ever been more relieved, ever wanted something more than in that moment. Consuela rolled her tongue around his exposed helmet then took it into her mouth, gripping his erection lightly with her lips as her tongue continued to circle the end of it.

Consuela's head rose and fell, taking more and more of him into her mouth until finally her lips closed round the base of his shaft.

'Oh God,' Ricardo thought. 'This is it, deep throat—this is really it!' Consuela pulled back up to the top of his cock and resumed the slow descent, inch by inch, to its base.

She was incredible. He'd never had head like this. Consuela kept him hovering perpetually on the brink of coming. Her lips and her tongue doing just enough to maintain the bliss without ever pushing him over the edge.

Ricardo glanced up at the sky. The clouds had moved in and darkened it. 'It might even rain,' he noted and then marveled at himself. 'What a stupid thing to think at a time like this.'

Consuela took him as close to an orgasm as he could possibly bear without tipping over and took her mouth away. Ricardo's legs tensed and he thrust upwards, humping the air above him, coasting the edge of a climax.

Consuela let him settle down then took hold of him again. She straddled him and placed his cock between her labia. She rubbed herself slowly up and down his erection without letting him inside her. She pressed the end of his cock against her clitoris and began to bring herself to orgasm.

Being so close to entering her without being inside her was another exquisite torture and he thrust upwards, trying to penetrate her as she moved against him. She put a hand on his chest to still him then continued with her private orgasm.

Consuela started to groan as she approached her climax, a full throated groan that seemed to travel up from deep inside her. Then, on the cusp of coming, she slipped him inside herself and slid right down the length of his cock, enveloping him, drawing him deeper and deeper inside her. She was warm and tight but incredibly wet. It felt indescribably right to be inside her.

She arched her back and pushed herself down on his cock, tilting her pelvis till she found that sweet spot she needed. Her legs and hips started to shake as the orgasm built inside her like a depth charge. She roared as it hit, moving through her body like an electric current. Then she collapsed onto his chest, spent and panting.

The early evening air cooled and little drops of rain began to fall, breaking the humidity. Far off in the distance there was a slight rumble of thunder. Ricardo took advantage of Consuela's collapse to roll her over onto her back and sink himself inside her. It was his turn now.

Consuela smiled. She was going to let him take control. Ricardo pushed into her with quick hard thrusts and she moaned her delight. For a brief moment it occurred to him that he should put a condom on. But there was nothing at hand and he wasn't going to stop. He didn't want any kind of barrier between them. He wanted to leave his come inside her. To penetrate her, meld with her, and join their bodies completely.

The sky lit up briefly overhead, like a bright sun beam breaking through the clouds or the searchlight of a low flying plane. Ricardo hardly noticed it. He was too intent on coming, on Consuela, on her wetness and warmth.

Then came the deafening, bone shaking crack. It was the sound of the sky breaking, of the air fracturing, of the storm ejaculating into the ground. But Ricardo and Consuela were in its path. All they knew was the crack and the flash. The blinding flash that shook them as the sky discharged itself into their flesh.

Then blackness.

CHAPTER 9

RICARDO LAY STILL, in mounting agony, until he was sure the bear had gone deep into the forest. His coccyx was raw and throbbing. The pain was getting to be more than he could bear. Consuela's muscles were hardening. Rigor mortis was setting in and her arms and legs were locked around him. She was weighing on his chest and restricting his breathing. He had to move.

Ricardo put his arms around Consuela's cold body and tried not to look at the damage to her face. He rocked her corpse gently back and forth, wincing from the pain in his coccyx and his loins. When he'd built up enough momentum he rolled her body on to its side and then over on her back. The torment this caused him was almost balanced by the relief it brought to his blistered backside.

He needed to get out of the forest and back to his jeep. No one knew where they were and it was too remote to hope a hiker or a group of girl guides would find them. He had to move himself and Consuela or he'd die out there.

Consuela's arms were locked about his in a dead, stiffened embrace. He had to push them apart to free his own arms without moving so violently he'd tear the seared flesh on his abdomen. Consuela's rigid, lifeless muscles cracked and popped like snapping twigs as he prized them apart.

When he had enough room, he reached up past her head and dug his fingers into the earth. He pulled Consuela's body along the ground with his arms and pushed her with his crotch at the same time, using his feet to give him leverage. This caused him intense discomfort, but he moved forward a few inches.

He could do this. It would work. He could get back to his jeep and get them to send an ambulance. Ignoring the throbbing ache in his groin he dug his fingers into the ground and tried again, pulling with his arms and pushing with his crotch. They moved a little further this time and Ricardo picked up a head of steam.

Soon they were out of the clearing and into the forest. This posed new problems. Most notably when Ricardo found a huge oak tree in their path. He had to reach out with his left arm and pull them to one side so they could go around it, inching forward then moving back round to the right when they'd cleared it.

The ground ahead was on a gentle slope. He was moving up hill, grabbing roots and earth to pull them forward and bumping Consuela along with his crotch in a grim parody of their former passion. The evening before she'd been soft and warm and he'd been desperate to lose himself inside her. Now she was cold and stiff and he was desperate to separate himself from her corpse.

Flies began to buzz around the shredded flesh and torn skin of Consuela's face. A milky eyeball looked as if it was about to fall out of a socket that no longer had eyelids. Ricardo could see her exposed teeth. They were yellow and crooked and several were missing at the back. Consuela hadn't had great dental care. He could see her hardened dried up tongue behind them. He tried to forget that he had recently put his own tongue in that rotting mouth, and in other cold, dead places that now held him trapped.

To take his eyes off her face, Ricardo scanned the trees and the scenery for landmarks. He was looking for something to orient himself, to work out the route back to the jeep. It wasn't easy. He hadn't been paying much attention when they'd come through the forest earlier. His mind had been on other things. He wasn't even certain how far they'd come.

At least he could see better thanks to the early morning light breaking through the branches. Had he really been in the forest all night? Ellen would be really worried now. Oh God what was he going to tell her? It's not like he could hide anything. The evidence was clamped round his cock.

It wasn't a strange number on his cellphone or unexplained scratches on his back. He had the charred and mauled corpse of a one night stand stuck to his body. That was a little hard to explain away. What was he going to say?

"Darling, you won't believe this but I was attacked by a Latino forest zombie and the only way to subdue it was to stab it with my cock. Then, and here's the funny thing, it just melted and now it's stuck to me." He started to giggle as he pictured Ellen's reaction. "Well darling, I did say that nothing would ever come between us, so what's a little decomposing-drug-smuggler between two people in love. All the same, I don't think we'll sleep on the good sheets tonight."

Ricardo couldn't stop laughing. It wasn't funny at all. He was scarred for life. He was facing death. But every time he looked at the raw, bloody pulp that was Consuela's face he just lost it. He couldn't stop himself, even though all the shaking tore at his wounds. He got so hysterical he lost control of his bladder.

He'd heard the phrase 'pissed myself laughing' many times, but he'd never actually experienced it until now. He felt the hot liquid flood the cold hard cavity of Consuela's uterus and surround his penis.

The hilarity drained from him along with the piss and he began to cry. Great wracking sobs shuddered up from inside him. He cried for the horror and the pity of his situation. He cried for his stupidity and the dreadful price he was paying for it. For all the secrets he couldn't swallow and had to drag through the forest instead, like the half eaten cadaver he couldn't shake off. His sins really had found him out and here he was, carrying them around with him, just like Ellen's Priest had said.

When he finished crying he felt totally wiped but also strangely relieved. He could face this situation and he could survive. His major priority was getting back to the car and getting medical attention. Once he'd sorted that out then he could deal with the fall out. Until then his primary goal was to stay alive and worry about the consequences later.

His sense of purpose renewed, Ricardo resumed his efforts, dragging himself and Consuela up the sloping forest floor. His progress was slow. It took him all morning and most of the afternoon to cover ground that he probably ran over in a matter of minutes the day before.

His arms ached and he had a permanent cramp right across his shoulders. The longer he kept moving the worse it got, but what other choice did he have? He couldn't afford to rest up, he had to keep going and push through the pain.

The raw, angry flesh around his loins was worse. It was trying to scab over but every time he moved he cracked and pulled at the hardening surface. Along his abdomen and across the tops of his thighs the wounds were leaking blood and yellow puss. The burned pork smell they'd been giving off became more putrid.

Ricardo had read somewhere that you could die of septicemia if you got dead tissue into your blood stream. He wondered if that included having your crotch stuck in a cadaver? Did that mean he was already dead. Was there any point struggling to get to a hospital? Could they do anything to help him now?

No. He had to stop thinking like this. It wasn't going to help him. While he was still alive there was still some hope. Medical science could do all kinds of things these days. They'd find a way to put him right.

Ricardo stopped for a moment to let the pain in his shoulders die down and to get his bearings. This part of the forest did not look at all familiar. He searched around for a tree, or a fallen branch or something that he recognized and found nothing. He groaned as he realized he'd gone off course. The trees were getting thicker which meant he was probably heading back into the forest and not out of it. He was going to have to turn around and retrace his route until he got back on course.

With a huge amount of discomfort Ricardo started to pull himself and Consuela back in the opposite direction. Turning her corpse around proved to be more difficult than dragging it. The ground was uneven and littered with branches, roots and rocks. Finally he got back on course and started heading in what he hoped was the right direction.

He got back to a part of the slope he recognized. There was the tree where he'd caught Consuela the first time and almost kissed her. He was coming at it from a different angle, that's why he missed it the first time.

This meant he was near the jeep. There wasn't much further to go. He just had to keep going a little longer and he'd be there. He could grab his phone and get an ambulance out there, or a helicopter to fly him to safety. This sudden realization gave him new resolve and, for the first time since he'd been struck by lightning, he was almost optimistic.

He dug his fingers in the earth, tensed his muscles and got ready to shift Consuela.

Then found he couldn't move another inch.

His limbs just wouldn't respond. All the energy had drained from him as though the earth, or Consuela, or something had simply sucked it right out of him. He was frozen. He couldn't move any part of his body.

Even Ricardo's head became too heavy to hold up and he let it fall forward onto Consuela's lifeless shoulder. He was too exhausted to move. He had no reserves of energy. He was spent and felt as dead as the corpse he was inside. Ricardo's mind kept telling him to push on. That it was only a little farther to go till he was out of the forest, but his body completely failed him and refused to move another inch.

CHAPTER 1 0

RICARDO S STOMACH LET out an anguished
groan. He hadn't eaten in over 24 hours and he'd
puked his last meal over Consuela. If he didn't eat
something he wouldn't be able to go on. There was no
food nearby. He wasn't one of those outdoor types who
knew how to forage for mushrooms and berries, even
if he was he wouldn't have the strength to find
anything.

The only thing to hand that even vaguely
resembled food was what remained of his last meal.
He could see a piece of ground pork nestling in the well
of Consuela's ear. Two kernels of sweetcorn were stuck
to the side of her neck and there was half a kidney bean
on her collarbone.

Ricardo stared at the tiny morsels of food for a
good five minutes before he found the resolve to do
what he had to. He told himself that he'd already eaten
the food once. All he was doing was putting it back into
his body where it belonged. That was all. There was
nothing gross about it.

Ricardo took a deep breath and put his lips to the
cold cartilage of Consuela's ear. He scooped the pork
into his mouth with his tongue. It tasted of rancid meat

and bile. He chewed and swallowed it anyway. He gagged and the pork threatened to come back up, but he took a deep breath and held it down. So far, so good.

He put his lips to her neck and pulled the sweetcorn off with his teeth. He tried not to think about planting kisses on that self-same neck when it was warm and had a pulse. Instead he chewed the tough, dried kernels that would have stopped any Green Giant from being jolly.

He did the same with the kidney bean and began to root around Consuela's face and upper body for any clumps of food he could find. After a while his hunger kicked in and he stopped worrying what it tasted like or whether it had once been a diced onion or a piece of tortilla. He just swallowed it.

When he couldn't find any more morsels he licked at the bitter, dried puke that caked her frozen flesh. His animal instincts took over and his brain shut down. He had to eat to survive and he couldn't allow himself the luxury of disgust. Couldn't stop to consider how low he'd sunk, sucking vomit from the half eaten face of a corpse.

As the regurgitated food hit his gut, Ricardo could feel it cramp with hunger. He was desperately in need of sustenance but there was no puke left on Consuela. The bear had eaten most of it before it had torn her face up.

Ever since the bear had left them, Ricardo had been trying to ignore the fraying chunks of skin and the exposed muscle that made up half of Consuela's face. Now he regarded it as the bear must have, with the eyes of a predator. And all he saw was food.

He sunk his teeth into the raw flesh of her cheek

and tried to tear at it like the bear. It was much tougher than it looked. The blood that coated the muscle had dried into a scab. He ran his front teeth over the tendons of her jaw and scraped off the dried blood and shredded muscle.

He wanted to hate himself for what he was doing. He knew he ought to feel disgust but he was too tired and hungry to feel anything but relief. It was just meat he was eating after all, no different from a pig or a cow. He'd never eaten raw pork but it probably didn't taste much different from Consuela. She was dead anyway, so why should she care? At least she was finally proving useful to him.

Once he'd finished, Ricardo could see the white of Consuela's cracked cheek and jaw bones. When help came, he'd tell them that the bear did all this. He lifted his hand to wipe his chin and found the life had come back into his arms. His legs were also working again. His stomach groaned, but only because it had food in it.

His shoulders and his forearms ached when he moved them. So did his calves and his feet, but Ricardo was only a little way from the safety of his jeep and he had the energy to get there now. All it took was one last little push.

The forest floor evened out and the trees began to thin as the road got nearer. Consuela's legs felt heavier on the backs of his thighs. Her arms were starting to move as Ricardo forced her along the ground. Tiny bubbles of blood frothed between her teeth and what remained of her lips. Rigor mortis was wearing off.

Christ, it's been that long? Ricardo thought. Consuela's legs went soft and flopped to the ground.

As her muscles relaxed she got heavier and harder to move. The skin around his thighs and stomach began to tear and weep even more.

The muscles of Consuela's crotch didn't relax though. He tried a couple of tugs to see if he could free himself but she still held him fast. Christ, what would it take to get her off him? She was worse than any limpet. Worse than any sin he carried around with him. What had he done to be punished like this?

The agony of moving Consuela was now so intense he could taste it, grind it like grit between his teeth. "Fuck you," he shouted in her face. "Fuck you and your dead limp body. You are not going to stop me. Do you hear me? You're not!" His arms were shaking. There was a painful knot between his shoulder blades that stabbed every time he pulled himself forwards, but he was not going to be beaten.

More light came through the trees up ahead and Ricardo was sure he could see the road. He was nearly there. He was going to make it. He wasn't going to die out here in the woods and be eaten by vermin. He was going to survive.

He laughed when he saw the road, and the sound scared him. It wasn't a happy or relieved laugh. It had an edge of hysteria and desperation to it. It showed Ricardo how close he was to losing it. How near he'd come to being broken by this whole experience.

The sight of the road gave him more impetus. He pushed on towards it but it wouldn't come any closer. Now that the end was in sight it was excruciating. The road remained the same distance away no matter how much he sped up. For a moment Ricardo wondered if it was a mirage. Perhaps he was hallucinating with all the pain. Then he felt gravel beneath his fingers and he was certain that he was near. The final leg of any journey is always the most interminable and he'd never wanted a journey to end more than this.

Ricardo put his head down and stared at the ground. He stopped thinking about the road, or reaching his jeep. He just concentrated on the dirt in front of his nose as it passed by, inch by tortuous inch. When the dirt turned to tarmac and sunlight hit the back of his neck he knew he'd made it out of the woods.

CHAPTER 11

RICARDO LOOKED UP and tried to find the jeep. It was nowhere in sight. He glanced up and down the road but there was no sign of it. Sweat broke out over his body. Where had it gone? Had it been stolen, or towed away by Park Rangers? He was dead if it had.

Then he caught sight of a broken boulder by the side of the road. He'd passed it just before he pulled over. He must have gotten turned around in the forest and come out further down the road. That's why he couldn't see the jeep. It was just around the bend.

Shit, he had to drag himself down the road to get to the jeep. Ricardo punched the road in frustration and instantly regretted it. Now he had to crawl to the jeep with sore knuckles.

Consuela's rigor mortis had completely worn off and the gases were starting to build up inside her. Ricardo could feel the bubbles swelling and breaking in her stomach. Must be all the drugs she swallowed. One more gross thing for him to endure. One more reason to get her off him as soon as possible.

The road was harder to move along than the forest floor. There was nothing for Ricardo to grip onto and the tarmac scraped the skin off his knees and his shins.

He had to keep shifting onto the verge and then back on the road when a bush or rock got in his way.

Consuela wasn't helping any either. Her flesh had gone limp, so not only was she heavier but her whole body resisted him. It was like pushing a giant bag of jelly that absorbed half of his momentum. A putrefying bag of jelly that stank of blood and pus.

The sun was behind the tree tops by the time Ricardo saw the jeep. It took him almost an hour to reach it, cursing and swearing at Consuela's stinking corpse the whole time. Dusk was fast approaching as he pulled himself alongside the passenger door.

The handle was too high for Ricardo to reach from the floor. He had to find a different way to get to it. He pulled his knees up under him and reached behind Consuela's back. Then he rocked himself backwards until he was kneeling up with Consuela's corpse sprawled over him. He had visions of the complicated positions he and Ellen had seen in a Joy of Sex DVD, except none of them had been with corpses.

Ricardo shuffled around until Consuela's back was against the rear passenger door. He placed his hands in her armpits and stood up, taking her with him. He grunted as the skin around his midriff tore, but he managed to prop Consuela's body against the jeep and pin her there with his weight.

Ricardo pulled the handle but the door didn't open. What the fuck was up with it? Why wasn't his keyless card working? Then it hit him. His card was in his wallet and his wallet was in his jeans back in the forest. No! This could not be happening. He could not get this far only to fuck up at the final hurdle. There was no way he could go back and look for his wallet, not after what he'd gone through to get here. He'd have to find another way into the jeep.

Ricardo glanced down at the verge and saw a small pile of rocks. He couldn't reach them from where he was. He'd have to move to where they were. He pulled Consuela's corpse away from the jeep then fell forward on to it, letting it cushion his fall. More skin tore round his crotch but he ignored it.

As he shuffled over to the rocks Ricardo felt the gases build up inside Consuela again. Like something was moving in her guts. Must be a split bag of coke or something. He reached the pile of rocks and grabbed a big jagged one. Then he maneuvered Consuela around so he could stand and pin her corpse to the jeep again.

Ricardo raised the rock to smash the passenger window and hesitated. He loved this jeep. It was a work of automotive art. Breaking the window was an act of desecration. He tried to think of other options but drew a complete blank. It was one more shitty thing he had to do in order to survive.

The glass scattered across the passenger seat as Ricardo reached in and opened the door, ignoring the shrill sound of the alarm. He pushed Consuela's body through the door and fell onto the passenger seat. Broken glass crunched beneath Consuela's cold, naked flesh as Ricardo pulled them into the interior and opened the glove box.

Ricardo pulled a heap of stuff out of the glove box and found his i-phone. He clicked the refresh button but the screen stayed black.

The battery was dead.

He found the lead to charge it, but without the

keyless card he couldn't start the engine and without the engine he couldn't charge the phone. Without a charged phone he was dead.

Shit!

Shit! Shit! Shit! Shit! Shit!

His whole plan to beat this situation depended on his i-phone and now his i-phone had let him down. He spent his entire life on that phone. It felt like he'd been betrayed by his best friend. For a long time he just stared at the phone with an open mouth, clicking the refresh button over and over, hoping that a tiny bit of charge might magically appear in the battery. Just enough for him to make one call. That's all it would take.

Why hadn't he charged the phone before he left home, or left it to charge in the car? Why had he let Ellen talk him into this dumb trip? Why hadn't he just left Consuela in that parking lot? Ricardo played the events of the last two days over in his mind, trying to correct every mistake he'd made, as though he could go back and change time through the simple power of his imagination.

He couldn't though. He'd tried everything and he'd failed. The futility, the sheer hopelessness of his situation hit home and Ricardo was done. He gave up. 'That's it', he thought, 'I'm finished'. He stopped fighting the inevitable. He let go and relaxed and his body went limp. All the resistance drained from his muscles and he became as flaccid as the decaying corpse his cock was still stuck in.

He wondered how long it would take him to die of blood poisoning. Which would get him first, that or the hunger? It would probably be the blood poisoning, he decided. He wouldn't get hungry considering what he'd done to Consuela's face and would probably do again when he got too desperate to stop himself.

He deserved to die. After what he did to Ellen and poor Consuela's corpse, he had no right to go on living. It was better this way. Ricardo just hoped it would come quickly so he could finally be rid of all the pain.

CHAPTER 12

TIME LOST ALL meaning. Ricardo stared into the foot well of the driver's seat, hardly blinking, until it got too dark to see.

A text tone chimed and a dim light came on in the foot well of the passenger seat. Ricardo blinked. The tone sounded again and the light flickered back on. It took Ricardo a while to recognize what it was. He'd given up on everything, including thought, and now his mind was taking a while to work out what he was hearing.

It was Consuela's phone. The shitty piece of crap she'd used to text her drug connection. She must have dropped it in the jeep and it had slid under the seat. It was a phone that worked. He was saved.

Ricardo pushed himself and Consuela just far enough out of the passenger door to reach beneath the seat and get the phone. It still had charge and a signal. He wasn't going to die.

Ricardo dialed 911. The phone cut out. He tried again and the phone refused his call. It was text only.

Ricardo only knew three numbers off by heart: Ellen's cell, his Mom's and his local Pizza delivery. He composed a quick text to his Mom:

'It's Riccy, need help badly. Send an ambulance to Coronado Forest, Route 5 off of Highway 19, pls, pls hurry!!!'

He typed in the number and pressed send. The phone wouldn't let him. He tried sending it again but the phone blocked him. He sent the same message to Ellen and hit another brick wall. Out of desperation Ricardo tried sending it to the Pizza delivery place and wasn't any more successful.

The phone would only let him text one number. The same number that had sent the most recent text and the other twenty unread texts before it. It had to be Consuela's connection. He'd given her a phone that only let her text him so he could stay in complete control of her. It made sense when Ricardo thought about it. If you were running drugs you wouldn't want anyone to know where your mules were. You'd want to make sure they could only get in touch with you and no-one else.

That meant Ricardo was going to have to get some guy he'd never met, who was very possibly a criminal psycho, to save his life, even though the guy would probably hold Ricardo responsible for Consuela's death and the loss of his drugs. Ricardo was going to have to play this very carefully. He opened the most recent text:

'Bitch u betta be runnin cuz ima kill u wen i catch u'

Great, the guy was pissed. This was going to be

worse than he thought. Ricardo pressed reply and wrote:

'sorry, ran into sum trouble, need help badly!!!'

The text tone rang almost immediately:

'damn rite u in trubble!!! i lost my buyer!!! u in deep shit!!!'

Fantastic, thought Ricardo.

'couldn't help it, sorry!!! stuck in Coronado, need an ambulance NOW!!!'

Ricardo stared at the time on the cellphone screen, counting down the minutes till the guy texted back. It took him six minutes to reply. It felt like sixty.

'no shit u need a ambulance, they bout ready to hatch now.'

What did he mean 'hatch'? He wasn't making any sense.

'what's about to hatch?'

'bitch don't be playin' me. wot d'ya think u swallowed?'

Ricardo was confused.

'drugs'

'pleez, u be dumber than i thought. they wuz eggs and u know it.'

'i don't understand'

'no u don't. i had me a buyer. wuz gonna pay top dollar for rare monitor lizards, banned in the US. all u hadda do wuz get the eggs here.'

'monitor lizards?'

'them things is flesh eaters and they be born hungry.'

Ricardo pushed his fingers between Consuela's teeth and forced her mouth open. He found the thin piece of twine tied around her back tooth and pulled at it. The twine came up easily, there was no weight on it.

On the end of the twine was a clear plastic bag containing pieces of blue speckled egg shell. There was a big hole in the bag. The edges of the hole were torn and ragged as though made by teeth that were tiny but incredibly sharp.

So that was the little secret that Consuela had swallowed. It wasn't drugs. It was something rare, dangerous and very expensive. A secret that had been waiting to hatch.

Ricardo felt more movement in Consuela's gut and realized it wasn't gas either. It was a secret brood with teeth so sharp Ricardo couldn't begin to imagine how they'd feel.

Then he didn't have to imagine anymore. Consuela's little secrets chewed through the wall of her abdomen, met his, and carried on.

All he could do was scream, and push at the corpse that held him fast until his damaged flesh tore and ruptured and bled. Because the pain from the teeth was worse than any he'd yet felt.

And Ricardo remembered what he hated about secrets. They had a way of eating you up inside.

TAKING THE PISS

SO I'M TAKING a slash in the King's Arms. The two blokes either side of me finish up then leave as I'm shaking the last drops off. I'm all alone.

I check the door, then crouch down in front of the urinal. It's one of those big stainless steel jobs, with a long trough at the bottom. I get right up close to the sluice, where all the piss runs, and I whisper, "Danny, I know you can hear me."

I know what you're thinking, but I'm not touched or nothing. I just hate Danny Taylor. He's always been a nasty streak of piss. One of those useless thugs whose lips have been glued to a crack pipe since they were fifteen.

Danny didn't have no dad around when he grew up see. That's cos his dad Charlie topped himself. Walked into his garage one night and started up his prize BMW. He loved that car more than his family. There was only one person Charlie loved as much as his car and that was Charlene, his bit on the side. But Charlene got tired of his shit and left him.

So Charlie got tired of life. He started up the engine and instead of getting a hose and sitting in the front seat, he went round the back of the car and put his mouth straight over the exhaust. Like he was blowing his prize possession. The pipe was so hot it melted his lips, fused them to the exhaust. He was a terrible colour when they found him several hours later. His lips glued to the pipe.

Charlene didn't go to the funeral, but she wore black for a week as a mark of respect. She's nice like that is Charlene. She just can't take men too seriously. That's why she can't stay committed to one. They've never been there for her so why should she be there for them. That's what she told me when she dumped me.

I fucked her for a while after Charlie died. Nothing serious, but I had a lot of fun and I was sorry when it ended. I was in her kitchen when she told me. She was wearing this long baggy top, not one of her usual tight, low-cut jumpers.

Maybe she was trying to make herself look less attractive so she could get rid of me. Or maybe she was hiding something. I don't know. But nine months later Stevie was born. Terrible shame about that kid, terrible shame.

The stench of the urinal brings me back from the memories. "Danny," I say. "No one can hear you mate, they think it's just the pipes."

I know a lot about the pipes in the King's Arms. I did a job for the landlord a few months back. The urinal was playing up. The sluice was backed up and the piss was spilling out of the trough onto the customer's shoes. So he got me to look at it.

Turns out there's a little crawlspace right behind the wall where the urinal hangs. That's where all the pipes are. I had to go through the yard at the back and knock through the outside wall to get to it, so I could clear the blockage.

Only two feet wide it was. Working in there reminded me of being in solitary. I did a bit of bird when I was a youngster, for fighting mainly. Thumped a guard when I was inside and ended up in the hole. Wasn't too different from that crawlspace, except it smelled better, even with all the dead rats.

That was the funny thing about the crawlspace. I think it was something to do with the air circulation or whatever, but all the rats were perfectly preserved, like mummies. Some of them must've been there for decades as well, but not one of them stunk.

I cleaned them all out when I cleaned out the sluice pipe. You wouldn't believe the shit I found in there. Great clumps of slimy pubes and other stuff you can't imagine, like a glass eye and a tiny baby doll's arm. No shit, a baby doll's arm, don't ask me how that got there.

I look at the sluice at the end of the trough and try to imagine how it would fit through the little round grate. "You shouldn't have done that to Stevie," I say. "You realise that don't you, Danny?"

Danny had persecuted Stevie his whole life. Maybe because of who Stevie's mother was. Or maybe because of the way he was born. He wasn't like other kids. His left arm was stunted and never grew. It remained the size of a baby's arm. Plus he had this weird lazy eye that used to go all over the place when you were talking to him. Made it difficult to look him in the face. It also made him a target for little cunts like Danny Taylor.

I tried to help him when I could but there's not a lot you can do when it's kiddie violence. If you cuff them round the ear you're likely to end up back in stir these days. Plus I wasn't around that much. All the same I did feel a bit responsible. Like I said, Stevie was born about nine months after me and Charlene split up, and even though Charlene had a lot of fellers, I've always had my suspicions.

The whole thing between Danny and Stevie came to a head about a week after I'd finished the job at the King's Arms. Stevie walked into the men's room and saw Danny at the urinal. He must have been scared, but fair play to him, he stepped up right next to Danny.

I'm not certain exactly what happened next. Maybe it was Stevie's arm, or maybe he'd had a few and couldn't handle it. Perhaps it was his sense of humour, but he ends up pissing all over Danny's shoes.

Danny was having none of that. So he took Stevie round the back of the King's Arms and did a number on him. Dragged him outside by his little arm. Stevie was howling with the pain as Danny damn near wrenched it off. Then he punched Stevie to the ground and started kicking him. Stevie lay there crying and saying sorry but Danny wouldn't listen.

He kicked all of Stevie's front teeth out. Then he put his foot so hard into the back of Stevie's head that his lazy eyeball popped out.

While Stevie lay there on the ground, in a pool of his own blood and piss, screaming for his mother, Danny stamped on the eyeball. Laughed as it popped open under his Nikes and ground it into the tarmac. When he was done, he pulled out his cock and pissed into Stevie's open eye socket. Then he went back inside and finished his pint. It was an hour before someone thought to call an ambulance.

The police asked around a bit afterwards, but no one round here talks to them and their heart wasn't in it. My heart was. I can feel it pounding as I crouch next to the urinal.

"You didn't think I'd let you get away with it did you, Danny?" I whisper. "There are some things you just can't walk away from."

He did think he'd walked away from it though, and he bragged about it to anyone who'd listen. I heard him one night down the King's Arms. Standing at the bar he was, proud as fucking punch, telling everyone how Stevie had it coming. "Taking the piss he was," that's what Danny said. Can you believe that? He reckoned Stevie was 'taking the piss'.

So I went home and got a hammer, a chisel and some super glue. Then I waited for Danny to leave the pub. Caught him on his way home. He was full of beer and soft as shit. Putting him down was a piece of piss, I'm not a defenceless wee lad like Stevie.

Then I went to work with the hammer and chisel. Not like you're thinking. I did take out Danny's front teeth, but that was later. First I went at those bricks I'd laid in the pub's outside wall. Shame really, I'd done a bang up job on them, but I made good when I was done and you'd never know I opened that crawlspace again.

That's where I left Danny, lying on his side with his wrists and ankles bound. That's where I used the superglue.

"You know what Danny?" I whisper, keeping an eye on the door in case someone comes in. "I read somewhere that the human body can survive for up to two months if it has a regular supply of liquids."

I picture him lying there, just like his dad, with his lips glued to a pipe. But unlike his dad he'll take a long time to die. Cos Danny's lips aren't glued to an exhaust pipe, they're glued to the sluice pipe from the urinal.

"Taking the piss, Danny, that's what you said about little Stevie, do you remember? But now you know what it's really like to 'take the piss'."

THE CASTIGATION CRUNCH

SUNDAYS WERE A real bitch in Hell. God rested on the seventh day of His world building spree, so His Angels were always on a 'go-slow' when it came to processing new arrivals.

This meant the 'can't pray, won't pray' brigade got shunted downstairs without any chance of a reprieve. Even those with otherwise spotless records. No last minute change of heart for them. No 'haven't I got egg on my face, do let me recant'.

They didn't even get to stop off at the first level of Hell (otherwise known as 'I Can't Believe It's Not Heaven') where the virtuous non-believers usually landed. First pointed out by the poet Dante and now the initial stop of his Inferno tour bus as it made its weekly rounds of the 'Homes of the Kitsch and Heinous'.

All this meant a huge increase in the daemon Ashmodial's workload. The squat, hump-backed brute had spent the morning arguing with a group of new arrivals who felt it most unjust that they were going to spend eternity being tormented in a fictitious construct to which they were ideologically opposed.

One of them even had the gall to try and bribe him. A naked bookish wretch by the name of Humphrey Suchs. "You can't buy your way out of Hell," Ashmodial told him, his stunted wings flapping in annoyance. "This is eternal damnation. See the clue there is in the name. It's eternal, it doesn't stop for anything, definitely not money. There are some things that don't have a price, 'specially when you're dead. I can see you're a fish out of water here. This is not a place you're going to recognise, Suchs."

Ashmodial wasn't surprised to find the scoundrel was an economist. A profession that practically guaranteed you a place in Hell. Most economists were sent to the fifth level sector where Marx and Engels presided. Here they were forced to apply crippling regulations to a moribund market in order to feed and clothe a growing army of poor and indigenous people. Ashmodial had something different in mind for the wretch however.

Suchs was stretched out over a lava filled crater in the Seventh level when Ashmodial next saw him. His wrists and ankles were bound with razor wire so taut his limbs were popping out of their sockets. Flesh eating larvae burrowed their way under his charred skin but he still seemed pretty cheerful.

This disconcerted Ashmodial. He was just reaching for Suchs' notes when they were snatched from him. He rounded on the individual responsible only to find it was his boss Lucifer. This was all Ashmodial needed, a surprise inspection by the top brass. This Sunday wasn't getting any better.

Lucifer had come in his formal aspect, complete with cloven hooves, horns and a pointed tail. He even had the pitchfork he carried when greeting visiting dignitaries. Ashmodial was puzzled as to why he'd gone to such trouble.

"Humphrey Suchs," said Lucifer. "It's not often that we get a sinner of your stature in Hell. Economic adviser to world leaders, best-selling author and personal guru to fading rock gods, we are honoured to entertain you."

"Actually," said Suchs. "I'm rather glad you've got a copy of my résumé, because I have a few propositions I'd like to run past you."

"You want to proposition me? You have some gall, Suchs. Your economic reforms caused untold suffering to millions of innocent people."

"My point exactly, just consider what I could do down here, given the right opportunities."

"I'm listening," said Lucifer.

***

A month later Ashmodial was accompanying Suchs as he showed Lucifer the results of his first set of reforms. Lucifer arrived in his Dark Gentleman aspect. He was done out in formal evening wear and carried a gold handled cane. His jet black hair was slicked back and the only daemonic concessions he made were a pointy goatee and tiny horns.

Ashmodial wasn't sure quite why he'd been chosen as Suchs' personal assistant. When Lucifer had set Suchs free and put him to work, Suchs had pointed to him and said, "I want that daemon to come along as my personal assistant. In fact I insist upon it." Ashmodial wasn't sure if Lucifer agreed because Suchs had insisted or Ashmodial had done something that really, really annoyed him. If it was the latter then Lucifer couldn't have hit on a better way to punish him.

"And now I want to show you what I've done with the DR department," said Suchs, his blistered skin now covered by a coarse hair shirt. Lucifer raised a quizzical eyebrow. "DR department?"

"Daemonic Resources, it's the new name for personnel. Under the previous regime we had an average of five daemons tormenting every soul. This was extremely inefficient and hardly cost effective. A systemized downscaling of the workforce means that we now have one daemon to every five souls. Contracts are issued under a system of competitive bidding meaning that only the most sadistic and aggressive daemons are now working in the field and the SYI is up a record breaking twenty five points."

"The SYI?"

"Suffering Yield Index, another of my recent innovations allowing us to quantify the exact amount of pain and misery we're causing at any one moment."

"And how has the rest of the workforce, as you dub them, responded to your reforms?"

"Not very well," said Ashmodial. "They've gone on general strike."

"A very fortuitous turn of events," said Suchs. "If a daemon actively refuses to harm a damned soul then this can only be construed as an act of kindness. And an act of kindness, as you know, is the only transgression a daemon is capable of making. This means that every infernal entity engaged in this industrial action can therefore be reclassified as a sinner and, as we know, all sinners are subject to Hell's eternal wrath. In a stroke the tormentors become the tormented and the number of victims under Hell's dominion has undergone a fourfold increase."

Before Lucifer could make any comment they arrived at the entrance to Hell. What had once been the most thriving and bustling section of Hell was now a desolate wasteland. "What's happened here?" said Lucifer. "Where are all the—"

"Admissions staff?" said Suchs.

"Yes," said Lucifer. "What have you done with them all?"

"Sacked," said Ashmodial. "Every one of them."

"Not every one of them," said Suchs. "I've maintained a skeleton crew to man the gates every third Thursday."

"But the backlog of entrants will be immense," said Lucifer. "It could take years to get into Hell."

"More like decades," said Suchs. "And the paperwork they have to do beggars belief. This is the one innovation that I'm most proud of. As you're no doubt well aware, the most excruciating thing about any form of torture lies in the anticipation. In fact this is often so terrible that the actual torture often comes as a relief. Previously the damned learned of their fate within hours of arriving. Now it can take up to twenty or thirty years and the whole time they're caught in a bureaucratic nightmare that's positively Kafkaesque in its proportions. Can you imagine the torment they're going to go through?"

Ashmodial saw Lucifer do something he very rarely did—smile. "I'm impressed Suchs, very, very impressed."

***

"Haven't you finished yet?" said Suchs, adjusting his frayed tie and smoothing the ill-fitting suit jacket that covered his hair shirt. Ashmodial was struggling with a tangle of USB cables. "I don't really know what I'm doing," he said. "I've never seen a lap-top before. I didn't even know we had them in Hell."

"That's because you don't keep abreast of the latest developments in torment and damnation. If you did you'd know there's a whole department on level four where miscreants with a fear of public speaking are forced to give Absolute Power Point demonstrations on subjects they know nothing about for all eternity. Now hurry it up, I'm due to outline my plans to corrupt the entire afterlife any minute."

"I don't see how you're going to corrupt the entire afterlife with a Power Point demonstration."

"Not a Power Point demonstration, an Absolute Power Point demonstration because, as everyone knows, Absolute Power Point corrupts absolutely."

Before Ashmodial could reply Lucifer strode into the space and seated himself behind the large boardroom table Suchs had procured for the presentation. He was sporting his Fallen Angel aspect. His hair fell in golden ringlets about his face and he carried the now extinguished torch that had once won him the title of Morningstar.

"So what have you got for me today?" Lucifer said. Suchs clicked his fingers. Ashmodial killed the lights and switched on the projector. The slide on the screen behind Suchs showed a map of all the levels and domains of Hell. "Now as you know," said Suchs, "Hell is divided into nine levels. Each one overseen by an Arch Daemon and devoted to punishing a specific set of sins."

"Is there a point to this?" said Lucifer.

"There is." Suchs clicked through to the next slide which showed a graph of an exponential growth curve. "Each level of Hell expands in a direct ratio to the number of souls it houses. Hell however is an eternal state, so it should be exempt from the normal rules governing time and, most importantly, space. Why then is Hell limited in its size and influence by the number of souls it contains?"

"Do you have another way of determining its size?"

"I do. What I'm proposing is the formation of a Future's Market." The next slide showed three fat daemons each squatting on a large pile of souls and exchanging great wads of cash with each other. "If you multiply the percentage of souls that commit each individual sin by the projected population growth, you arrive at a fairly accurate estimate of the future size of each level of Hell. So why not allow those levels to expand to their estimated sizes in lieu of their future population. You can also allow the different levels to trade in this new real estate, determining the value by the fluctuations in sinful behaviour. In periods of economic growth, for instance, Greed is at an optimum, while in a recession Envy receives a welcome boost."

"And what would be the eventual outcome of this scheme of yours?"

Suchs clicked on to the final slide showing, a diagram of an enormous Hell dwarfing a tiny little Kingdom of Heaven. "Hell will not only become the largest and most powerful territory in the afterlife, but you and the ruling elite will become fabulously wealthy."

"Suchs, I like the sound of that. I like it rather a lot."

***

Ashmodial struggled up the steep stone steps with the scalding hot massimo latté. He didn't want to think about what he had to go through to find one in the depths of Hell. He spent a lot of time trying not to think about what he was going through at the moment.

At the top of an impossibly tall, gothic tower he knocked at the door of Suchs' corner office.

JASPER BARK

"Come," shouted Suchs as Ashmodial pushed open the heavy wooden door. The back walls of the office were made entirely from glass. The view was unimaginable. The panorama of Hell that lay beneath showed all Suchs' reforms in their terrifying glory. Ashmodial didn't recognise Hell anymore.

Suchs, dressed in a bespoke Oswald Boateng suit, was chatting to a client on his hands free headset with his feet up on a huge antique desk. Ashmodial was still agog at Suchs' ability to track down luxury items in Hell.

Being an economist, Suchs had grasped one of the basic principles of Hell, that envy and covetousness are better ways of tormenting people than they are of motivating them. For the damned to suffer from constant envy there had to be items for them to covet and more importantly others who owned those items instead of the damned. This one brilliant insight had brought Suchs power, influence and a coterie of daemonic disciples.

He motioned for Ashmodial to put the cup down on an ivory coaster. The tower shook and Ashmodial spilled the latté. Suchs glowered as his client droned on. Before Suchs could discipline Ashmodial there was another larger tremor. Footsteps sounded on the steps outside and the door burst from its ancient hinges.

Lucifer was standing in the doorway. He had come in his most terrifying and Vengeful aspect. His huge frame looked as if it was carved from living brimstone. His body was cloaked in smoke and flames and lightning crackled in arcs between his large, curved horns.

"SUCHS," he bellowed. "Hell is in ruins!"

"I'm going to have to put you on speaker phone," Suchs said to his client as Lucifer stormed towards him.

"Thanks to your ridiculous policies we've expanded our territory to the point where we can't find most of the damned. If we can't find them we can't torture them and the whole of Hell reverts to a paradise. All nine levels are in imminent danger of collapse."

"Well, you have to remember that it is a bull market."

"Don't talk bull to me." Lucifer grabbed him by the throat. "Do you know what Hell is built on, what makes up the fabric of its existence?"

"Well it's a complicated issue, to begin with you have to cross reference the SYI with the—"

"It's not a complicated issue! It's suffering, eternal suffering plain and simple. If people stop suffering Hell falls apart. What we're facing is a major Castigation Crunch and there's only one way out."

"And what might that be?" Suchs was sweating and his suit was on fire, but he didn't look as rattled as he ought to be.

"It's what's known as an Aeternas Excrutiatum, what in your terms we might call a Baleful Bail Out. To get rid of such a toxic deficit in our despair the one soul responsible has to suffer 700 billion times more than any soul has ever suffered."

"Is that right?"

"It's the only way out of the slump in our suffering. What I'm personally going to do to you is going to a 700 billion times worse than what Simon Cowell does to the trouser leg."

"So in essence, what you're saying is that I'm worth 700 billion souls to you."

"And a whole lot more."

Suchs squirmed in Lucifer's grip and turned towards the speaker phone. "You heard him boys." There was a flash of heavenly radiance and a portal opened up in the room. An Archangel and two angelic aides strode through. "What is the meaning of this?" said Lucifer. "This is my domain and you're making an unwarranted intrusion."

"We are about God's business," said the Archangel. "And that requires no warrant or permission."

"I'm afraid I worked out a little counter deal with the CEO of your rivals," said Suchs.

"The Lord rejoices in saving even the lowliest souls," said the Archangel. "But is especially pleased with one worth 700 billion."

"Wait a minute," said Lucifer. "Do you mean to tell me you're here to redeem Suchs and take him back to Heaven with you?"

"Indeed we are."

"But it doesn't work this way. There are rules. You know as well as I do he has to do something pure and good enough to make up for all the evil things he's done."

"Putting the whole of Hell in imminent danger of collapse. That sounds more than pure and good enough to me."

"But he caused untold damage to the lives of millions with his reckless free market policies."

"And you put him in charge of your finances," said one of the Archangel's unimpressed aides. "That was a smart move."

The aides took Such's arms and led him towards the portal. "No," said Lucifer. "I will not allow this. This sinner cannot leave Hell."

"You have no say in the matter," said the Archangel. "It has already been decided by a higher power than you."

Suchs stopped in front of the portal. He turned and pointed at Ashmodial. "Wait, I can't leave without my assistant. I want him to come too. In fact, I insist upon it."

"I was afraid you might say that," said Ashmodial as one of the aides grabbed him by the hump and marched him to the portal.

He didn't want to go. Lucifer was about to explode with rage and rain liquid agony down on anything in his proximity. But even the prospect of escaping that fate didn't make Ashmodial eager to step through the portal.

***

After an hour in Heaven Ashmodial found himself longing for the liquid pain of Lucifer's wrath. The piety, the self-righteousness, the endless choirs, it was like someone had taken an industrial sander to his scaly hide.

The long white robe they were all obliged to wear hung round his misshapen body like a shroud on a dismembered corpse. Suchs on the other hand had somehow managed to get Gianni Versace to hand stitch his. He smiled his predatory smile at Ashmodial as he hopped along the clouds towards him.

"I hate it here," said Ashmodial. "You know that don't you?"

"Oh come now Ashmodial," said Suchs. "This is the Eternal Reward. You should be grateful I plucked you from the fires of Hell."

"What fires? Hell's bankrupt and can't afford the

79

fuel to keep its fires going. Why should I be grateful that you brought me here? Why did you do it?"

"To prove a point. You told me the afterlife was a place I wouldn't recognise. You told me I was a fish out of water. So I turned Hell into something you wouldn't recognise. Then I brought you to Heaven. Now who's the fish out of water?"

"Look Suchs, whatever it takes, whatever you want, just tell me and I'll make sure it's yours. But please, you've got to get me out of here."

"Are you trying to buy your way out of Heaven? I thought you told me that some things don't have a price, especially when you're dead. I think I've rather proved you wrong there. Here endeth the lesson."

Suchs turned and strode away from him, kicking up little wisps of cloud as he went. "Wait Suchs," Ashmodial called. "You can't leave me here, you just can't. It's not right, Suchs . . . "

But Humphrey Suchs was beyond appeal. He had his arm around an elderly angel with a long white beard who was stationed by the pearly gates. "Now look, Peter," he was saying. "I've been meaning to have word with you about your admissions policy . . . "

ILL MET BY MOONLIGHT

אמונה
J Moran

"**AND WHAT MAKES** you think I've finished with him?" Helena slid her fingers down Ben's stomach and stroked his cock.

Ben placed a hand on her arm. "I think he's had enough. You've worn him out."

"Oh really, that's not what he seems to think." Helena was right. His cock was most definitely hard between her fingers.

"What a traitor," Ben said. Helena laughed. She'd once told him that a woman has two relationships with a man, one with the man and the other with his cock. Maybe they'd been talking behind his back, but right now his cock was on Helena's side.

She leaned over and brushed his chest with her lips, then kissed her way down to the cock she so was expertly stroked.

"I'm a bit sticky," Ben said. "Are you sure you want to do that?"

"Well if you enjoy the taste as much as you say you do, I don't see why I shouldn't."

Helena ran her tongue lightly up the length of his shaft, from the root to the tip and then blew on it. "Are you sure I've worn him out?"

"I think he's found his second wind."

"Good."

Helena circled the end of his cock with her lips. Hovering, mouth open, at its tip, teasing him. It was working. He bit his lip he was so desperate for her to continue.

Just as his longing got to be unbearable, she took him in her mouth. She pulled back his foreskin and rolled her tongue over the sensitive flesh beneath. She pressed down with her lips and took more of him in her mouth.

Helena went slowly at first, drawing out the pleasure. As her lips and tongue increased their rhythm the pleasure built, Ben felt himself swell in her mouth.

He could still smell her on his face and fingers. He lifted a hand to his face and breathed in her scent. He hadn't been lying about loving the taste of her. She was the best of all his lovers. Except for Judith of course.

Helena moved faster and took Ben deeper into her mouth. He was coasting up to the edge of his second orgasm when Helena took her mouth away. He sighed his displeasure but Helena just laughed, reached out and dug her fingers into a pot of face cream by the bed.

She took a big gob of the cream and smeared it around the end of his cock. The cream was cold after the warmth of Helena's mouth but it wasn't unpleasant. Helena rubbed the cream around the end and down the length of his shaft. Her slippery palm and fingers kept him hard.

Ben was wondering what she had in mind when Helena raised herself up and straddled him with her knees. She took hold of his cock and guided it between the cheeks of her butt.

"Oh my God," he said. "Really?"

Helena smiled. "I want to know you in every way possible before I let you go."

Ben smiled back, but only to hide his suspicion. Was there some hidden meaning to that last comment? He couldn't always tell with Helena.

His suspicions faded when he felt her puckered hole open to let him in. It gripped his cock, warm and delightfully tight. Ben thrust upwards in his excitement and a pained expression crossed Helena's face.

She placed a hand on his chest to stop him. "Wait," she said. "Let me get used to you. It's a bit painful if you go too hard at first."

Ben relaxed and sank back on the bed. Helena slid down him till her buttocks pressed against his thighs. Her intense green eyes were hooded with desire and her brown, shoulder length hair fell around her face, still messy from bed.

Ben caught her gaze. There was a shared moment of illicit excitement, of forbidden thrills and delightful violation. She rocked her hips as she got used to the feel of him inside this new part of her and welcomed him further in.

Helena put her middle finger in her mouth and wet it with her tongue. Then she reached between her legs and found her clitoris. Her hips moved faster as she began to bring herself to orgasm.

Ben wasn't far off himself. He tried to hold himself back to let Helena come, but she was riding him fiercely now and he was losing control.

Helena's shoulders shook as she forced herself onto him, taking him further into her. Her hand moved quickly between her legs and she let out a deep moan.

Ben felt his orgasm start at the soles of his feet. It raced up his legs and engulfed his whole body. He almost had an out-of-body experience as he came, leaving his body along with the sperm that he shot deep inside Helena.

There was a timeless moment of bliss that seemed to stretch forever and just as Ben was coming down from it, Helena reached her own peak, arching her back with a welcome sob that became a full throated cry. Her head fell forward, her shoulders dropped and as the last of her orgasm washed over her she collapsed on his chest.

Ben held her to him, panting as the last of his climax subsided in waves of diminishing pleasure. He was soft now and shrinking inside her. Helena rolled off him, leaving him with a feeling of regret and relief.

"Methought I was enamoured of an ass," Ben said, quoting A Midsummer Night's Dream. "Oh good, sweet Bottom," Helena replied, countering his quote with another.

With Helena no longer on top of him, Ben took the opportunity to slip out of the bed. "I'm sorry," he said. "It's late and I have to get back."

He was completely spent and the post coital urge to flee was starting to assert itself. Helena rolled over. "Well you better go then," she said, lighting a cigarette with her back to him.

Ben scanned the floor. Where had he thrown his boxer shorts? On second thought he'd better leave them off, considering where he'd just been. He wandered through to the bathroom. No time for a shower, best he just wash himself in the sink.

He heard footsteps as he was lathering his crotch. "And back to Athens shall the lovers wend," said Helena leaning in the doorway. Another line from A Midsummer Night's Dream. He wiped the soap suds off his mouth and chin. "Removing every trace of me?" she said. "Is this what you do before you go back to her?"

"I . . . err, didn't mean for you to see me like this. Sorry, I guess it's a bit insensitive isn't it? I'm not trying to be rude." He smiled. "Take the sense sweet of my innocence." More lines from the play.

"Lysander riddles very prettily," she countered, keeping up the game. The play had become the secret subtext of their brief affair. It was how they negotiated their way round the infidelity.

It was also a method of controlling him. Helena was older and more educated, but not as sexually confident as him, in spite of her surprise performance this evening.

They'd met in a bar where he liked to hang out. He'd seen her around quite a few times before that and knew she was checking him out. He'd played it cool and waited for her to make the first move.

When she did he found that she'd learned quite a lot about him. He was kind of flattered by this. He knew his 'bunny boiler alarm' should have been ringing but she was smart and sophisticated and didn't seem the stalker type, plus she knew how to be discreet. Discretion was essential. He didn't want his partner Judith finding out.

Helena worked in the theatre. She knew of a big production of A Midsummer Night's Dream that was being cast. She thought he'd be a natural for one of the lovers. She offered to coach him for the audition. He had no experience but she thought he had natural talent.

It was a come on, an excuse for them to meet. He was half-hearted about the acting but whole-hearted about the sex. Unlike the acting, he had a lot of experience at that. He was getting better at the quotations, but that was still her speciality and she never let him forget it.

He headed back to the bedroom to dress. Helena followed him. "So far be distant; and goodnight sweet friend," she said, slipping her arms around his shoulders and leaning in for a kiss. She pushed her crotch against his cock but she wasn't going to get any response out of it this time.

Her lips were sloppy and he tried to avoid her tongue. He could smell the stale sweat on her armpits. He'd had his fun and wanted out of there as quickly as possible.

His usual tactic was to fake sympathy. To flash his beautiful brown eyes and pretend he hated to leave. A few drawn out kisses on the way to the door would then lead to a hasty exit. Helena wasn't having any of it. Something in her manner suggested it wasn't going to be so easy tonight.

She'd given the impression she was building up to something the last couple of times he'd seen her. He thought for a moment it might have been the anal. Now he was wondering if he was right to be suspicious earlier.

She left him alone to dress but she was waiting for him at the door. She'd found a skimpy silk robe and had freshened her make up. He didn't like the lipstick she was wearing.

He took a deep breath and leaned in for a kiss. She placed a finger on his lips and stopped him midway. Then reached up and placed a kiss on each of his eyelids whispering, "Churl upon your eyes I throw, all the power this charm doth owe."

He reeled and for a moment it felt like he lost

consciousness. He was still on his feet when he came to seconds later and heard Helena say, "Lysander, if you live, good sir awake."

"And run through fire I will for thy sweet sake." He had no idea why he said that but as soon as he did he realised he was hopelessly in love with Helena. He hadn't a clue how it happened. It was like being hit by a thunderclap. As it said in the play, 'brief as the lightning in the collied night', but just as sudden and irrevocable.

Helena smiled, obviously pleased with herself. "And what of Judith?"

"No, I do repent the tedious minutes I with her have spent."

"Good," said Helena. "Then you're finally going to tell her you're leaving aren't you." Was he? He loved Judith. He couldn't remember when he'd decided to leave her, but suddenly it seemed inevitable.

"It'll kill her," he said. "How do I tell her? I don't think I can." He felt a mounting sense of panic. It was all happening so quickly. One minute he was trying to make a quick getaway, the next he was planning to leave Judith. Helena came to his rescue with a quote, "For aught that I could ever read, could ever hear by tale or history . . . "

" . . . the course of true love never did run smooth."

"You know what the secret is?"

"No."

Helena leaned in and whispered in his ear. "Sacrifice. Make certain you tell her that." She kissed his cheek, opened the front door and saw him out.

***

He drove home in a daze. Normally after he'd been

unfaithful all he could think about was getting home to Judith. All he wanted was to be close to her. To smell her hair and taste her skin. To wash away all the intimacy of his other lover.

Up until a moment ago he'd loved Judith above every other woman. Like it was hard wired into his flesh. Written into the spiral helix of his DNA. He'd believed that the molecules of his body were held together by her love. It was the breath that animated him. He came alive at their first meeting. His friends laughed when he said it, but he honestly couldn't remember a time before her.

Now that it was all over he still couldn't fathom why he was so compelled to see other women. Maybe being with Helena would change all that.

He hoped it would but he feared there was something within him that would always crave the touch of another woman. It was intoxicating being intimate with a person that you hardly knew. Perhaps he was looking for some form of validation.

He needed to be desirable. To see himself reflected in the shallow pool of someone else's lust. It staved off the feeling he often had of being insubstantial. The fear that his whole identity could just crumble and fall apart at any moment.

He wasn't certain if cheating made him happy. Or if he even enjoyed it half the time. He knew it would destroy Judith if she found out just how unfaithful he'd been. He never had less than three other women on the go at any time. The relationships were short and soon lost their novelty but there were always plenty more to take their place.

It was all very well being faithful when you hardly

got the chance to cheat. When the closest you came was a sly glance from a work colleague, or a drunken fumble at the Xmas party. But when someone makes eyes at you every time you leave the house, it becomes more difficult. The temptation was constantly there. At the supermarket, on the bus, out at a bar with friends, someone would always catch his eye, start up a conversation and find a way to leave their phone number with him. Could he change for Helena? Would she still want him if he couldn't?

Or would she act like Judith? He could swear that on some unspoken level Judith had given him the go ahead. Had willed him to do the things that would hurt her most. It wasn't anything she said or did. It was just . . . it was something in the way she loved him. Some slow burning resignation that practically pushed him into it.

Was he wrong for blaming his faults on Judith? Did it make him a coward? Was he lying to himself? He tried to remember how he'd been in other relationships. Was this a pattern? Every time he tried to recall he just drew a blank. Why did he have this block? Maybe he didn't want to remember. Or perhaps there was some brutal truth that lay at the end of that line of questioning. A truth only Judith presided over.

He felt for the lump at the root of his tongue. He always did that when he started to go off the rails. Whenever that dizzying feeling of vertigo came over him. When he felt like he'd pushed things too far and everything was slipping out of his grip, he was suddenly aware of the weight of it. Like he'd just shaken it loose.

He'd been meaning to get it looked at. Whenever

he mentioned it to Judith she smiled and told him it was nothing to worry about. She was always doing that. Acting like she had all this secret knowledge, it was kind of irritating. Now that he was in love with Helena he was irritated by a lot of things Judith did.

***

He pulled into the parking lot when he got home and sat holding the wheel, staring straight ahead for nearly an hour. He felt as though he'd been watching himself from a great distance ever since he left Helena's. Like he wasn't in control of himself. Was that love? If it was then why wasn't he overjoyed? He never felt this way with Judith.

He was starting a new life with Helena so why did breaking up with Judith fill him with dread? Did he honestly think he couldn't exist without her? "Not Judith but Helena I love," another line from the play. "Who would not exchange a raven for a dove?" Saying it aloud gave him the courage to get out of the car.

He knew something was wrong the minute he set foot in the living room. For one thing Judith was up. She was never awake at this time of night. He was the night owl. She was the early riser.

She was sitting on the edge of the sofa in the living room, wearing a nightie and a woollen cardigan. Her long auburn hair was tied back with a scrunchy and she was wearing her reading glasses.

The light was off and moonlight streamed in through the front window. She didn't say anything when he entered. She looked tense as she stared into her mug of herbal tea, as though she were getting ready to do something she couldn't put off any longer.

"You're up," he said, hovering in the doorway. His

mind was racing for something to say. He'd decided to leave but he hadn't thought anything through. How should he handle the situation? Was it better to be sensitive about the whole thing or just blurt it out and be done with it?

"Look," he said. "There's no easy way to say this, so I'll be blunt. I'm leaving you. I'm in love with someone else and I'm going to be with her."

Judith looked up in surprise. She obviously hadn't expected him to say that. She was staring at him with a mixture of annoyance and disbelief. It was the sort of look she had when a piece of software she'd written had malfunctioned.

It wasn't the response he'd expected. He searched for something to say. What was the last thing Helena had said to him? "It's like it says in the play I'm rehearsing, 'the course of true love never did run smooth', what it takes is sacrifice, do you see?"

All of a sudden she did see. She got off the sofa and switched on a table lamp then came and scrutinised him. She scanned his face like she was looking for a programming error. She spotted his eyelids and rolled her eyes.

"I might have known." She produced a tissue, licked it and rubbed at his eyes like she was cleaning a child. He tried to step away but she grabbed his collar and held him still. "You've been charmed," she said as she removed the lipstick traces.

His vision blurred, his stomach churned and his legs went from under him. Judith caught him and helped him sit down. He started to come back to himself. What the hell had he just done? What was he thinking?

"Charmed?" he said. "What do you mean charmed?"

"When she kissed you on the eyes she put you under a spell. That's why you thought you wanted to leave me."

"I don't know what you're talking about. No-one kissed me on the eyes. I told you, I was . . . " The look on Judith's face stopped him dead.

Why on earth was she suddenly talking about spells and charms? She was a software engineer, what did she know about magic? Then again he had been acting really strangely since he left Helena's. Could she really have hexed him? How the hell did Judith know? It might explain why he just told Judith he was leaving her for another woman. Oh my God! Suddenly it hit him. He'd just admitted to being unfaithful.

His mind flailed about for some excuse, some lie that would dig him out of the hole he was in. Could he tell her it was an effect of the spell? No, then he'd have to admit to being with Helena. Every excuse he thought of crumbled into empty words before it reached his lips. For the first time in their relationship he was suddenly very frightened of losing Judith.

He looked into her cool blue eyes and knew he couldn't talk his way out of this. She was implacable. There was no more pretending. There were no honeyed lies that would smooth this over. They both had to admit to the truth. He looked down at his hand and saw it was shaking.

Judith switched off the lamp and went back to the sofa. "I suppose it's my fault really," she said after a long pause. "I know that's what women always say, but it is."

"N-no," he stammered.

"We take the blame for everything that happens in a relationship." Her tone was thoughtful now, there was even a wistful edge to it. Was that a good sign? Maybe this didn't have to be the end. Perhaps they could still find a way to work everything out.

"It's like the whole relationship is our responsibility so if anything goes wrong it's our fault. We know exactly how a man is going to act if he gets the chance to be unfaithful. So we take control of the relationship and make sure he never gets that chance. If he's the constant, we have to be the devious variable.

"If he does cheat it's because we weren't paying enough attention. We should have seen how smartly he dressed when he went out. We should have followed our instincts when we heard the way he said another woman's name, not told ourselves to stop being so silly. Then we wouldn't end up blaming ourselves when he does what we were expecting all along.

"I know we beat ourselves up about these things and blame the other woman. And I know that lets men off the hook far too much. But this is my fault. Men are like projects. You don't find Mr Right you make him. You find the best material you can and you go to work. There's always an unfortunate liking for sandals, atrocious table manners or a lack of ambition you have to fix. That's half the fun of it I suppose. That and showing off our handiwork when we're done. And that's always our down fall isn't it. Some other bitch comes along and reaps the benefit of all our hard work."

She stopped for a moment and stared out of the window. A tear welled up in her eye and almost seemed to sparkle as it caught the moonlight. She brushed it away and turned back to him almost smiling. He couldn't think of a single thing to say.

"I had to have a man who was attractive to other women. I wanted a trophy. I thought I could make the perfect man, but my vanity got the better of me, no not my vanity, my lack of imagination. You see, because I knew what men were like I thought I could make one from scratch. But knowing what they're like stopped me from seeing what they could be. I was too caught up in what you looked like, in the appearance of my creation. And that tainted the working."

What did she mean 'tainted the working'? She wasn't making any sense. Judith looked down at the damp tissue she was still holding. "I suppose I have to forgive her really, even with everything she's done. You see the thing is, I know she was acting out of love. Everything she ever did was out of love for me. I imagine she wanted to check out my handiwork as well. I'm sure she enjoyed you. I did make you rather a good lover, even if I say so myself."

Ben had no idea what Judith was talking about. Maybe it was the grief. It affected people in different ways. He couldn't talk to her when she was acting like this. Perhaps there were other ways to get through to her.

She patted the sofa and he came and sat beside her, but she wouldn't let him put his arm round her. She stroked his cheek, her fingertips soft and damp with perspiration. He started to get aroused. He knew he had to relax and take it at her pace though. To 'be in the moment' as she called it. "Poor Ben," she said. "I'm going to miss you."

"You don't have to miss me. It doesn't have to end just because . . . "

She put her fingers on his lips to quiet him, tracing each one with her fingertips. He parted his lips and she slid them inside his mouth.

His heart began to beat faster, as much with hope as arousal. They were going to make love. The relaxed and relieved sort of love that you make when you know it's all over but you just need to fuck. Then afterwards maybe she would fall asleep in his arms. Then when they woke perhaps she'd realise what it was they nearly lost and they'd find a way to bring it all back again.

Judith pushed her fingers under his tongue and took hold of the lump there. It was kinda painful. He winced but didn't pull away. She was playing rough was she? Well that was okay, he could go with kinky. Anything so long as she came round.

The lump started to move. This startled him and he jerked his head back. She took hold of his chin to stop him from moving and forced his jaws open wide. Then she pulled the lump out of his mouth and held it up for him to see.

It was a shiny stone tablet. What the hell was that doing in his mouth? How long had it been there? He peered more closely at it. It had four letters written on it.

As soon as he read them he knew it was a mistake.

EMET

It was a Hebrew word. He didn't know why but he knew it meant 'truth'. He also knew everything was over. That was the 'truth' it revealed to him. He'd seen the magic word and now he'd turned to stone.

That's what it felt like. The last thing he was aware of was a cold sinking feeling in his gut. It seemed to seep out into his whole body, numbing it as it spread. He tried to stand and get out of there but he couldn't. He was paralysed. How could looking at a word do that to him?

The life just drained out of him leaving his flesh stiff and lifeless. He couldn't feel anything. His body was suddenly separate from him. Like a hollow, brittle shell he was rattling around inside. It seemed as though he was looking out of a mask that was about to be removed. Judith smiled with sympathy.

"I know this must all be strange to you but in a moment you won't feel a thing. I'd forgotten how miraculous the whole process is. I mean clay and straw coming to life, it's astonishing when you think about it—what you can do with the Kabbalah. It isn't all that different to programming really, with all its sacred combinations of words and numbers."

"It says in the Talmud that if the righteous wished to create a new world they could do so. All it would take is a different combination of the ineffable names of God. I wanted to build my own private world around my perfect man. I'm not the first to try it. The Rabbi Judah ben Bezabel made an artificial man as far back as the seventeenth century. Eleazar of Worms preserved the secret formula. I had to memorise twenty three folio columns and master the alphabets of the two hundred and twenty one gates. I recited it over every one of your organs. Do you realise what an act of love that was? And look how it all turned out."

She turned away from him and looked down at the small stone tablet she still held, turning it over in her hands. His mind was still fighting against what was happening. Maybe she'd drugged him, that's why he couldn't move. She could have put something on the tissue she used to wipe his eyes. Or was it Helena who'd done this to him? Had she slipped him some sort of truth drug? Was that why he'd confessed to Judith?

Oh God, what was he going to do? He couldn't feel anything. Was it an overdose? Was that what he was experiencing? Helena must have slipped him too much. He needed to get to a hospital. Why wasn't Judith doing anything to help him? Had she gone over the edge into some psychotic break from reality? There was something seriously wrong with him. Couldn't she see that? He was going to die if she didn't help him.

"She told me it would turn out like this," said Judith. "That's the ironic thing. She's no master of the Kabbalah, but she still knew. I suppose she's always been intuitive that way. Not that I paid much attention at the time. I'd given up on trying to perfect anyone else. I was too busy perfecting myself. That's the real purpose of following the Kabbalah. That's why I was trying to make the perfect man. I fell a long way short didn't I. But then I'm a long way short of perfection myself. I could never commit you see, just like you.

"I ran away from the person I truly loved to create someone who would do the same thing to me over and over. That's what I meant when I said it was my fault. Your infidelity came from me. I tainted the spell and I got to learn what it's like to be on the receiving end."

Ben was so frustrated at not being able to talk. This had gone beyond a joke. He could feel himself slipping away and she was spouting all this nonsense. He would have smacked her in the mouth if he could. Maybe it would have knocked some sense into her. He was getting desperate.

Did she really believe everything she was saying? Could there be any truth in it? You couldn't make a person out of straw and clay and magical alphabets could you? Of course not! He was real, he knew he was. He could prove it. He had thoughts and emotions and memories.

He cast his mind back for some memory of his life before Judith. Try as he might he kept drawing a blank. He couldn't remember a life before Judith because . . . because he'd never had one. He couldn't deny it any longer. She wasn't lying. She was showing him the truth.

Judith held the stone tablet in front of his eyes again. Then she rubbed away the first letter. Ben picked out the remaining letters in the moonlight.

MET

Which means death.

There was no point fighting it any more. He just had to let go and accept it was going to end. He felt his personality start to crack and drift apart like the fragile crust on a stream of lava. He began to see where the different parts of his identity had come from, each one borrowed from a friend, a lover and even her father.

"The minute you mentioned sacrifice I knew who'd done this. And I knew why. She wants me back. She's forgiven me but she needs me to understand where I went wrong. That's why she seduced you and sent you back. 'Sacrifice is the path to true love', that's the last thing she ever said to me."

Ben took one last look at the stone tablet. 'Ill MET by moonlight,' he thought slipping away like the echo of a prayer in an empty temple.

His last thought was from the text that undid him. A creature brought into being by sacred texts and destroyed by the removal of a single letter.

Judith placed a kiss on his empty lips. "Helena is my true love. She always has been. And you, sweet Ben, are my sacrifice."

HOW THE DARK BLEEDS

Moran

$\mathbf{T}$HE SCALPELS WERE so sharp Stephanie could almost taste them.

It had taken her a while to steal a full set. The long ones were the hardest to acquire. The surgeons notice when they go missing.

She arranged them in order of size for the tenth time that night, laying them out on the bare floor of the basement room. It used to be an auxiliary boiler room but they gutted it when they modernised the hospital's plumbing. Now it was empty apart from a few supply boxes. The bare walls hadn't been painted for over two decades and the only light bulb had been smashed.

Stephanie had brought a flashlight. She wasn't ready to let the darkness into the room. The darkness didn't threaten her, but what waited there did. Presences that thrived in the darkest hours and places.

The urge to use the scalpels was growing. Stephanie couldn't hold out much longer. She felt dizzy with longing as she picked up the shortest scalpel and thought about how it would feel slicing through her jugular.

Stephanie's heart beat faster and to hold back the yearning just a little longer she pressed her index finger onto the blade. It sliced through the layers of skin and a thick red trickle of blood ran out. She could feel the presences in the dark draw closer as she let the blood spatter on the concrete floor forming a tiny pool.

Stephanie shone the flashlight on the little red

pool. Maybe it was because she hadn't eaten in a day or more, or perhaps she really was losing it, but Stephanie was sure she could see pictures reflected on the surface of the blood. Images that swam in and out of focus like sediment rising from the bottom of a disturbed pond.

The images looked familiar. She stared harder, willing them into focus as she realised what they were. They were scenes from her life. Not memories, because she was watching herself from the outside. It was a disconcerting feeling, like watching yourself on video, or hearing how your recorded voice sounds for the first time. Her life was being played back to her stripped of all the self-serving misconceptions that so often colour our memories.

There was a word for what she was experiencing but Stephanie couldn't quite remember it. She'd had a conversation about it just recently, she was sure. Maybe the images in the blood would remind her. She stared hard as a scene began to form, a scene from her recent past.

Stephanie saw herself on the hospital wards, in the ICU . . .

***

Stephanie's uniform hung awkwardly about her. She could never find one that fitted. They were always too small or too large for her.

She tried to adjust it surreptitiously as the Duty Nurse briefed her. Stephanie nodded without paying too much attention. She was supposed to sit with someone on a suicide watch.

The patient had suffered third degree burns from a house fire. Her father had died in the fire and the

106

patient had tried to take her own life, so she had to be kept under constant supervision.

Stephanie sat down beside the patient and smiled politely. The patient gave Stephanie a cursory glance and then went back to scowling at her book. She was thin, with close cropped brown hair, olive skin and elfin features. She seemed to be repressing an intense, twitchy energy, as though there were something inside her trying to scratch its way out.

Her right arm and shoulder were covered with heavy dressing. The dog eared paperback she was staring at was The Living Goddesses by Marija Gimbutas. There was a pile of similar textbooks and faded hardbacks by her bedside.

"Good book?" said Stephanie. Without looking up the patient said, "Her work's largely dismissed by the most academics and she makes too many unwarranted assertions, but her views on the origins of religion are worth consideration."

"But you're enjoying it, right?"

"This isn't the sort of book you read for enjoyment."

"No I don't suppose it is. Are you a student then?"

The patient put down her book and stared straight ahead, not bothering to hide her irritation. "You know, none of the other nurses asked so many questions."

"I'm not like the other nurses."

The patient smiled and turned to look at Stephanie for the first time, gazing right into her. "No, you're not are you," she said, implying something Stephanie couldn't quite grasp.

"My name's Stephanie by the way, I didn't catch yours."

"It's Jan."

"Pleased to meet you. I'm sorry if I ask too many questions. I like to make time for people that's all. The other nurses might be caught up with their workloads but I like to find out what's going on. You wouldn't believe the things I've seen, that they miss. The people that have just walked in here, right under their noses."

"Oh I think I would."

Jan relaxed, and her mood thawed. "I'm not a student, but I was doing a PHD a few years ago. My Aunt brought my old books in, I'd left them at her house. She hopes I'll pick it up again, to take my mind off what happened."

"What did happen?"

"I'd rather talk about my PHD."

"Of course, sorry. I'm not an academic, but you could try explaining what it's about."

"Well it was supposed to be about 'Negative Depictions of Femininity in Pre-Rational Goddess Culture', or that was the title at least. It ended up being about the Heolfor."

"The what? Is that a foreign word or something?"

"It's ancient Anglo Saxon. It means gore or blood spilled in anger, but it might have a deeper meaning, one whose roots go back to an almost forgotten myth." Jan pulled an old book out of the pile by her bed and turned to a passage. The print was too small for Stephanie to read. "The first definite mention of the myth is in the Nine Herbs Charm, an Old English spell to treat infection and poisoning. It says 'These nine herbs have power against nine horrors, Against nine venoms and against nine poisons: Against the red venom, against the running venom, Against the blood that walks in woman's form, in sisterhood compact.'"

"Okay, you're beginning to lose me."

"That's okay, I'm not done yet. There are a few other mentions in Anglo Saxon writing, including suggestions that the Heolfor were around before even the Celts got here. The next important reference to the Heolfor is in the Malleus Maleficarum." Jan rifled through another book and pointed out a replica of a woodcut title page. "It's Latin for 'Hammer of the Witches'. Basically it's a handbook for hunting and persecuting witches written in 1486. At one point it tells the story of Marie Van Stratten, a woman who claimed her blood was bewitched and was desperate to be free of her so it could join the Heolfor. She claimed her blood was speaking to her and begging her to slash her wrists so it could escape her body. She disappeared soon after on the night of a new moon."

"Why a new moon?"

"Ah, now this is where it gets interesting. Have you heard of Edward Kelley?"

Stephanie smiled to herself and turned away so that Jan wouldn't see. She poured a glass of water so Jan wouldn't wonder why she'd moved. Some patients could be so taciturn to begin with, but get them on the right topic and they'll pour their heart out.

"You should drink this," she said handing Jan the glass. "Your throat sounds dry. Should I have heard of Edward Kelly?"

"Not necessarily," said Jan, putting down the water without touching it. "He was an alchemist and a spirit medium who hung out with Dr John Dee, Queen Elizabeth I's court magician. They used to speak to angels by scrying."

"Scrying?"

"Basically Kelley used to stare at a polished black stone till he had visions. These angels would speak to him and Dr Dee would write down what they said. One of the things the angels told them about was . . . "

"Let me guess—the Heolfor."

"Give the lady a gold star. According to Dee and Kelley, the Heolfor represent the worst aspects of femininity and are governed by the dark side of the lunar goddess Monanom. She was a strange minor deity, a bit like the Roman god Juno. A lot of goddesses have like a threefold aspect, they're both a maiden, a mother and a crone, representing the three stages of a woman's life... I'm not boring you am I? I have a tendency to go on a bit about this stuff."

"No, no it's really interesting, carry on."

"Okay, so Monanom only has two aspects, the maiden and the crone, and they're joined back to back like Siamese twins. The maiden is in love with the sun god but she has to hide the dark crone from him. For this reason her love is a chaste love and everyone sees her as the ideal woman while her hidden sister has to live in darkness, hidden from the sun where she can work her evil deeds. Everyone hates and fears the crone but loves and worships the maiden."

"Yeah, I've got a sister like that, loved by everyone."

"Thought you might," said Jan, giving her another penetrating look. Stephanie looked down at the floor, embarrassed and unnerved. Sensing this, Jan flicked to another page in her book.

"So, anyway, the maiden aspect of Monanom inspires women to be faithful daughters, wives and mothers. The crone lives in darkness, she's strongest when the moon is new or hidden and she inspires madness, betrayal and murder in women. The moon is supposed to affect the tides and the blood, especially menstrual blood. So the crone's servants, the Heolfor, are composed of blood, because that's what she has most control over."

"So, they're like vampires then?"

"No, vampires feed on blood, the Heolfor are made entirely out of blood and nothing else. Or as Dr Dee wrote 'blood that taketh on the human form and walks as to a woman's carriage.' They were said to bewitch the blood with their song and drive people to hideous acts in the darkest hour of the night. Some scholars have suggested that this is the origin of the concept of 'bad blood' and also why early physicians were so keen on bloodletting to release bad humours."

"You have read a lot about this haven't you?"

"Told you I was obsessed."

"Were there lots of these Heolfor?"

"There were nine. That was an important and magical number to the Anglo Saxons. Each of the Heolfor represent a different type of aberrant female behaviour, a bit like Jungian archetypes, if you know about that."

"A little."

"There was one that represented the worst type of wife for instance, one who betrayed her husband, slept with his enemy and had him killed. Or the worst kind of mother, who slaughters her child, the worst daughter who disobeys and murders her father. That sort of thing. This doesn't freak you out does it? A lot of people get all funny when I talk about it."

"No, not at all, it actually makes a lot of sense to me, strangely."

"Excuse me," said the Duty Nurse. She was standing right next to the bed holding a clipboard, but Stephanie hadn't seen her come up. "I've just been going through the staff roster and I can't seem to find you . . ."

***

Stephanie closed her eyes to stop the vision. She didn't want to see anymore. The rest of the memory was tedious and she was happy to let it end there.

So scrying was the word she was looking for. Was that what she was doing with the blood? Stephanie wasn't seeing any angels though. She wondered if Edward Kelley ever saw dark visions from his past. Things he hadn't told Dee about.

She stretched her back and shifted onto her haunches because her knees were sore. The flashlight flickered, its beam dimmer. The batteries were starting to go. She couldn't hold the dark at bay much longer.

She couldn't keep her eyes off the pool of blood either. Stephanie leant forward and gazed at it. An image of her reflection swam to the surface. Only it wasn't Stephanie's reflection as she was now, it was a reflection from the past. A transparent reflection in the window of a ward. A window through which Stephanie was watching Mike . . .

***

He had his back to her and he seemed worn down, stooped and a little older. Stephanie couldn't stop herself feeling a twinge of satisfaction. Maybe if he hadn't left Stephanie for her own sister he might not be so sad.

Stephanie had been three months pregnant when Mike left. She miscarried soon after. It had happened at three in the morning. Stephanie had phoned Mike as she sat on the loo, screaming at him as the blood poured out of her. Mike had claimed he was at his mother's at the time, the liar.

Stephanie felt mean going over those memories though. Mike was looking at his child in an incubator. The tiny infant boy was six weeks premature. Mike had a right to be sad and concerned. Anyone in his position would be.

Stephanie usually avoided the Neonatal ICU. Today she'd decided to visit. She hadn't expected to see Mike here. She hung back, uncertain of what to do, not wanting to make things awkward.

Mike looked lonely. Her sister was nowhere to be seen. That was probably just as well. Stephanie didn't think she could face her at the moment.

Stephanie's sister had plotted against Stephanie her whole life. She made a point of stealing what Stephanie prized most, especially when Stephanie was a teenager, that's when her sister stole their parents' love. She'd been having mental problems and they had to take her out of school for a while.

Stephanie spent long hours in her bedroom, wearing the same nightie for weeks on end, listening to her sister play up to her parents downstairs. She was being the perfect daughter that Stephanie could never be. Her parents never looked at her sister with the same weary disappointment they reserved for Stephanie.

It would make Stephanie so angry that she'd scream at her mother when she came in to change the bed sheets or try to coax Stephanie into a clean nightie. Her mother and father responded to these fits with a tired resignation.

Stephanie knew her sister was making the most of

the situation. Soaking up the extra love and attention until finally there was none left for Stephanie.

Things got a little better when her sister went away. That's when Stephanie started taking her pills and seeing a psychiatrist. Sometimes she would tell her psychiatrist how she felt when she pictured her sister at boarding school or travelling in Europe. Stephanie's psychiatrist would always try and discourage her from thinking or talking about her sister though. So Stephanie never told how she fantasised that her sister and seven others were secretly plotting her downfall.

Mike also discouraged Stephanie when she told him about her sister. He encouraged Stephanie not to dwell on her or what happened in her past. Then one day, without any warning he just up and left Stephanie for the one person who had stolen everything from her.

After what seemed like ages staring at the incubator Mike turned round, without any warning, and caught Stephanie's eye. Stephanie froze, she couldn't just turn her back and walk away. She had to face him. He was wearing the same look of weary resignation that she used to see on her parents' faces. That was her sister's doing. That's how she made everyone look at Stephanie eventually.

Mike stepped out into the corridor where Stephanie had been watching him. He hadn't shaved in a couple of days, there were streaks of gray running through his dark brown hair and his deep brown eyes looked watery and bloodshot. He appeared to have shrunk as well. He was never tall at five foot nine, but with everything weighing on his slumped shoulders he seemed to have lost two inches in height. Stephanie hoped her sister was happy.

"Stephanie . . . I . . . " Mike said, letting the sentence just trail off as though there were so many things he wanted to say that he couldn't pick one. "How is he?" said Stephanie, pointing to the incubator.

"Haven't you been in to check yourself?" said Mike. "When was the last time you looked?"

"Look Mike, please, I don't want to argue with you. I understand how you feel. I don't want to add to your grief." Mike looked surprised. "You understand how I feel?"

"Well obviously, do you think I'm stupid?"

"No, no of course not." Mike's tone changed. He became more conciliatory. "That's good, it's really good that you understand, it's a good sign." A tentative affection crept across Mike's face and he reached out and took Stephanie's hand.

Stephanie hadn't felt his fingers wrapped around hers for such long time it was a shock. She felt both joy and loss at the same time. Sometimes the simplest displays of emotion are the most honest. Stephanie's defences melted and she remembered why she loved Mike and how fierce that love was, in spite of everything he'd done.

"Stephanie, could you . . . could you do something for me?"

"Of course," said Stephanie. Mike pointed to the incubator. "Something that would really help him, and me . . . and your parents." Stephanie began to feel uneasy at the mention of her parents. Her unease only grew as Mike reached into his pocket and she heard a familiar rattle.

Mike pulled out a bottle of pills. "Please start taking your medication again." Maybe it was because he reminded Stephanie how her parents tried to cajole and control her. Or maybe it was because he had taken complete advantage of her emotions, but Stephanie lost it. She knocked the bottle out of Mike's hand and it shattered as it hit the wall, scattering capsules all over the floor.

"Fuck you," she shouted. "You had me feeling something for you and you threw it back in my face. Stop making this my problem. I'm sorry for what's happened Mike, but you left me for my own sister. Stop trying to dope me with tranquillisers because you hurt me!"

Stephanie turned to leave and Mike grabbed her wrist to stop her. "Stephanie I've spoken with Dr Connor and your parents . . . " Stephanie tried to punch Mike in the chest to make him let go. He held up his palm and caught her punch. "Fuck you," she cried again.

"Stephanie please, you're in danger, great danger . . . "

***

Stephanie put her hands over her eyes and pushed her head back so she didn't have to watch anymore. The blood was playing with her. It knew she didn't want to see these things.

Even though she knew how each scene ended she couldn't stop looking. She couldn't tear her gaze away until the very last moment. There were things she didn't want to admit to, not yet.

The blood was aware of this, it had to be, it came from her body. Was it playing with her? Did it need her to admit something before it . . . before it . . . Stephanie didn't want to finish that thought either.

She was trapped between things she didn't want to

remember and things she didn't want to think. Her eyes dropped back to the pool of blood. Another image was forming. She was in uniform again and back in the IC . . .

***

Stephanie hadn't been back to the ICU since her run in with the Duty Nurse. She'd found it was best to steer clear of certain parts of the hospital sometimes, until things cooled down and the staff there forgot about you.

Stephanie preferred to fly below the radar and not draw too much attention to herself. There was always something to keep you busy on the wards so it was easy to blend into the hospital without being bothered by the staff.

All the same, Stephanie had to risk the ire of the Duty Nurse to come back and check on Jan. She'd seen a lot of patients in distress while she'd been in the hospital. She knew many nurses remained detached and kept a professional distance. But you can't stop everyone from getting under your skin, you wouldn't be a good nurse if you did.

Stephanie was shocked when she saw Jan. She wasn't just slumped against the pillows propping her up, she'd sunk into them. Jan seemed to have lost an alarming amount of weight. Her skin was the colour of wax, and there were dark rings under her eyes. Her short hair was matted into brown clumps which stuck to her forehead with sweat. Her dressing had been changed but it was stained with perspiration.

Though she was hardly moving and just staring straight ahead of her, Jan still had that same twitchy energy, if anything it seemed to have intensified. The

117

vein in her temple was bulging and throbbing, all of Jan's veins were. It was like they were alive, writhing under skin so pale it was almost transparent.

Stephanie drew the curtains around Jan's bed and sat down. Jan barely registered her presence. "Oh," she said, after a considerable pause. "It's you." She hardly moved her head, just flicked her eyes in Stephanie's direction. "Is everything okay?" Stephanie said. Jan rolled her eyes and sighed. "Does it look okay?"

"No, I suppose not. Have there been complications with your burns. Did you get infected?"

"Not from my burns, they're not the problem."

"I'm not sure I follow you?"

"Really? You were my last hope. I thought you of all people might have understood, considering what you know."

"Jan, you're not making any sense. If you know you've got an infection you've got to tell the doctors, otherwise they can't give you the treatment you need."

"There's no treatment for what I've got."

"It's not A.I.D.S. is it? Because you have to tell the doctors about that. You could be putting other patients at risk."

Jan's chest started to quiver and her breath sped up. Stephanie thought she was about to have a coughing fit but then she realised Jan was actually laughing. "Oh Christ, you're in so much denial aren't you, it's so incredible it's almost endearing."

Stephanie bridled at this. "What do you mean? You think I'm in denial? I'm not the one hiding things from my doctors. You've got to tell them what's wrong with you if you've got an infection."

"They won't believe me if I tell them what's infecting me."

"Why on earth not? What is infecting you?" Jan turned to look at Stephanie for the first time since she'd come to see her. Her emaciated features made her eyes stand out, accentuating her piercing glare. "What did we talk about last time?

"Last time I sat with you? It was your PHD wasn't it? Moon goddesses, witch hunting and that guy Edward something or other . . . "

"Kelly."

"Yes, that's right."

"And what else?" Stephanie searched her memory. "Oh yes, the Anglo Saxon myth about the thingies—the heel . . . erm helio . . . ?"

"Heolfor."

"Of course, I'm sorry, it's not a name I'm familiar with, so it's hard to recall."

"Not after you know what I know it's not. Then it gets right into your blood."

"Jan, I'm sorry I'm not as clever as you, with your PHD and everything, but you're talking in riddles and I can't follow you. Has this got something to do with when you got burned, how you lost your father and tried to . . . erm . . . "

"Kill myself?"

"Yes, I err . . . I wasn't trying to be insensitive."

"Perish the thought."

"Do you want to talk about it? Will that help?"

"Help me or you?"

"I'm not sure what you mean—help you of course."

"I'm beyond help now."

"Don't talk that way."

"Okay, then let's talk about the Heolfor." Jan made a feeble gesture towards the books that lay unopened by her bedside. "My reading only scratched the surface of the myth. Most of my research was done in the field. I wanted to get a proper sense of where these beliefs came from. Why people needed to hold them. There are no precedents in other pagan religions."

"Really?"

"Oh yes, according to Austin Osman Spare, he's a 20th century artist and mystic, the idea of a being made entirely of blood is unique to Ancient Britain. Spare called them 'a living blood sacrifice, bound to the service of the moon's dark designs. A sinister sisterhood devoted to delirium and deviltry'."

"So how on earth do you do fieldwork on something like that?"

"You have to know where the Heolfor congregate and how such a sisterhood was said to manifest in these places."

"Places like what?"

"Anywhere blood is spilt and people take leave of their senses in the darkest hours, a battlefield, a site of slaughter and atrocity, even a hospital."

"Like this one?"

"Wasn't it you who told me about the things that take place here, right under the noses of people too busy to see them?"

"You did field research right here, in this hospital?"

"Did you know it's built on the site of the last great Pagan uprising in Britain? King Sighere of Essex and his army of followers were put to the sword here in 683 on the orders of Augustine of Canterbury, the Pope's emissary and the first Archbishop of Canterbury."

"How can you possibly know that?"

"There was an archaeological dig here when they

laid the foundations for the hospital. They found all the bones along with some pagan artefacts. Some of it's still on display at the local museum. But that's not all, in the eighteenth century they built one of the first British asylums here. It was burned to the ground in 1793 when the inmates rebelled and beheaded all the trustees with a makeshift guillotine in solidarity with the French Reign of Terror. This has long been a site of death and destruction, of dark, dark places that never lose the stain of delirium. What better place to search for the Heolfor."

"But you said they were a myth, right? You're talking as if they're real. I mean, you can't actually see a mythical being can you?"

Jan went very quiet at this and stared intently up at the ceiling. "I'm sorry," said Stephanie after a long pause. "I didn't insult you did I?"

"You asked me why I didn't tell the doctors about my infection. This is why. You're the only person in this hospital who might understand what's happened to me and even you find it hard to believe."

"Okay, I didn't say I didn't believe you, but I'm not actually sure what you're talking about. How can I believe you when you hide what you mean behind all these riddles?"

"You're right, it's a trust issue. People think I'm crazy enough without finding out the truth. That's why I keep them at bay with riddles."

"And to show them how clever you are."

"Well there is that."

"Please tell me what happened, I won't judge you."

"I wouldn't be so sure about that."

"You can trust me." Stephanie placed her hand on

Jan's. After another pause Jan said, "I've seen them—the Heolfor, right here in this hospital."

"You've seen them, where?"

"In the basement, there's an abandoned storage room, it's right over the spot where they found all the bones from the massacre. There's no light down there, which is why they like it. I studied the schematics of the hospital, I snuck in on a new moon and I went looking for them. There's things about them I didn't know though."

"What sort of things?"

"They're not immortal, they can die over time and they need new blood to replenish their ranks. They sang to me."

"Sang?"

"Stood around me in a circle and sang, seven of them."

"I thought you said there were nine."

"I told you they need to replenish their ranks, that's why they sang, it's how they infected me."

"By singing?"

"Directly to my blood. They converted it, harmonised it I suppose, made it one of them. Now it isn't part of me. It's fighting me to get out. Every time my heart beats my blood screams to be free, begs me to open up my veins, so it can be rid of me and join its sisters. That's why I'm on suicide watch."

"You think your blood wants you to kill yourself."

"Not kill myself, though I will die if it gets its way. It wants to leave me, to become something else, something deranged and malevolent, a blood being aligned to the darkness."

"What can you do?"

"I tried to fight back but I ended up here. Do you know what it's like to feel your blood turn against you, to develop thoughts of its own? To know that it's plotting your death as it moves through your body. I couldn't give in to it so I decided to poison it. I was walking in the woods near my home and I found a rotting badger. I picked it up, took it home and stuck a kitchen knife in it. My plan was to stick the knife in my body and give myself septicaemia. If I poisoned my blood then I'd kill the blood being, deny the Heolfor their new sister. I was standing at the kitchen sink with the rotting beast when my dad came in. We still share a house. He saw what I was about to do and he tried to get the knife off me. He probably thought I was having another of my episodes. I've had problems on and off since my mother died when I was twelve, that's why I still live with him.

"He nearly took the knife off me, but he's getting weak and old and I was angry. Angry that he'd try to prolong my suffering, try to stop me kill what was festering in my veins. So I lunged at him instead. He didn't expect that and the knife went straight into his chest. I remember the tiny 'clunk' the handle made as it hit his ribs. How he coughed and gurgled as the blood from his lung caught in his throat. He stepped backwards and reached for the kitchen counter to steady himself, but he missed it and toppled over backwards.

He reached out to me as he was lying there, slumped against the dishwasher. "Jan love," he said. "For God's sake, please . . . call an ambulance . . . please . . . " I looked at him lying there, crumpled pathetic and bleeding. This wasn't the man who'd raised me since my mother died. Who'd sat with me when I got ill, comforted me when I was sad and put a roof over my head. This was a vulnerable old man who'd just been infected with septicaemia. So I pulled the knife out of his chest and I rammed it into his left eye. He kicked a few times, went into spasms then he lay still. It was a mercy killing, that's what I told myself. Septicaemia is a hell of a way to die and I'd just saved him from that.

"I felt really cold after that. I couldn't stop shivering or keep my hands steady. I knew I had to hide the evidence and I knew I had to get back to this hospital. So I went to the garage and I got a can of petrol, then I doused the house and set a match to it."

Jan held up her bandaged arm. "That's how I got this. I think I was cutting off all ties to my past life, limiting my options so I couldn't avoid the inevitable. A neighbour called an ambulance and they took me here, like I knew they would. It's a new moon tomorrow night. I don't have much longer. I can't fight my own blood anymore. A police man came to see me this morning, full of questions and insinuations. It won't be long till they find out what really happened. But I won't be around to face them."

Stephanie had no idea what to say. Jan's story had knocked the wind out of her, like a blow to the solar plexus. "You told me I could trust you," said Jan. "Well, I have. I don't think you'll judge me either, because I think I know what you're planning to do. Even if you don't yet . . ."

****

Stephanie winced at the pain shooting through her palm. She looked away from the blood to her hand and saw that she'd stabbed herself with the scalpel to stop the vision. How much longer could she struggle with the blood before she gave in and saw what it really wanted to show her?

More blood trickled from her palm. She held her hand over the tiny pool and let the fresh blood add to it. It ran along her palm and down the length of her thumb, dripping from the tip into the pool.

Stephanie sighed, the release she felt was almost orgasmic. Her heart beat faster in anticipation, spurred on by the blood pushing its way through the organ. It sang in her ears, rising in volume as each drop joined the pool.

Stephanie's eyes drifted back to the pool as the drips rippled its surface, churning up new visions. Stephanie saw herself in a different part of the hospital. She was carrying a tray with blood samples on it . . .

***

The samples came from the children's Oncology and Haematology ward. They'd been taken from a child with MRSA. More tests were needed and a doctor had asked Stephanie to run the samples up to be despatched. As soon as she was away from the ward she knew what she was going to do. It was as if the doctor had handed her the plan along with the tray, it was that inevitable.

She stopped off to pick up a fresh syringe and headed down to the Neonatal ICU. With the recent cutbacks, it wasn't always fully staffed and during a shift change it could be unattended for up to twenty minutes. This was all the time Stephanie needed.

She stood over the incubator and gazed at her sister's child. She thought of the poor thing growing up in her sister's care. A woman who had robbed Stephanie of everything she'd loved. If this was the way she treated Stephanie, her own flesh and blood, then how much worse would she treat her own son?

Stephanie considered the abuse and neglect she'd suffered at her sister's hand. She couldn't let this innocent child fall victim to that. What sort of life would he have with that woman as his mother? Much better to show him mercy now than to inflict years of mistreatment on him.

He was so tiny and so frail, barely aware he was even alive. Would it be such a crime to take something from someone who hardly knew what they had? Especially if you were saving him from so much misery. He came from her bloodline, she couldn't turn her back on him.

Stephanie took the syringe out of the wrapper and filled it from the phial of infected blood. Her hands shook as she did.

She opened the incubator and stroked the head of the tiny boy inside. His eyes weren't able to open yet but he stirred and reached out for her. His fingers were so small they couldn't properly clasp Stephanie's little finger.

"Shh," Stephanie said. "It's okay, it will all be over soon." She pinched his little thigh until she saw a vein. He wriggled and let out a barely audible sigh of complaint, but she held him still and stuck the needle in his vein then pushed down the plunger.

Stephanie heard footsteps in the corridor. She quickly closed the incubator and left the room, dropping the syringe and the other blood samples in the bin on the way out. "God speed little man," she said over her shoulder and hurried out of the neonatal ICU.

Stephanie wasn't certain what to do with herself once it was all over. She felt a sudden need to speak about it, to unburden herself. She realised there was only one person to whom she could talk.

Stephanie went to look for Jan but when she got to the ICU her bed was empty. She asked one of the nurses on duty where Jan was but no one knew. The nurse said there was a shortage of beds so Jan had probably been moved to another part of the hospital.

Stephanie went back to the bed. All of Jan's books were still there so she couldn't have been moved. She asked around the other patients in the ward and none of them had seen Jan all day.

Stephanie began to get worried. She flicked through Jan's books to see if she could find anything that might give her a clue as to where Jan might be. She scanned the pages and the indexes, looking for any reference to the Heolfor, but she couldn't find one. The only mention of the word she found was in a collection of Anglo Saxon poetry which gave a brief translation of the word as: 'blood or gore'.

Stephanie remembered what Jan had said about encountering the Heolfor in the basement and decided that's where she must be. She made her way straight to the stairs.

The basement was musty. It didn't have the same sterile, disinfected smell as the rest of the hospital. The service corridors were like a low ceilinged maze. There was a constant throb and hum from the back-up generators.

It was more by accident that Stephanie found the door to the subbasement and made her way down the stairs. There was only one working light flickering in the corridor. Luckily, the hours she'd spent in darkened rooms as a teenager meant Stephanie had great night vision and her eyes quickly adjusted to the dark.

Stephanie turned a corner at the end of the corridor into complete darkness. She stumbled on with her arms outstretched until her eyes adjusted and she made out a door up ahead. As she reached for the handle the temperature seemed to plummet, as if the blood had drained from her body. At the same time Stephanie could hear a high pitched whistling in her ears.

The room on the other side of the door smelled of copper and salt. Stephanie was reminded of the taste of old pennies under the tongue. In the centre of the room was what looked like a discarded white sack. As Stephanie peered closer she saw that it was Jan's naked body.

Jan's throat and wrists had been slashed open. The cuts were deep and the edges ragged and tattered.

Jan's blood had pooled in a thick red puddle in front of her. Stephanie blinked when she saw something rising out of the puddle. It looked at first like long thin drips were running out of the puddle towards the ceiling, as though gravity had been reversed.

The drips were forming themselves into long, thin shapes. The shapes were sinuous and began to intertwine themselves, branching out like tiny underwater fronds as they formed a larger structure.

The structure seemed to be sucking all the blood from the puddle as it formed itself. The rivulets of blood were making the outline of a body, like a wireframe image. No, not a wire frame image, it was like a life sized map of the human circulatory system forming itself right in front of Stephanie.

Stephanie could see all the veins and arteries of a human body, of Jan's body, as the figure turned to regard her. It had no eyes, just the capillaries that would have flowed through an eyeball.

Stephanie recognised something of Jan in the hideous stare of this blood being. What she saw was the personification of Jan's unhinged fury. The deranged anger that had pushed a knife, soaked in rotting blood, into her father's chest, then killed him as he begged her for help.

Dark red stains were appearing on the walls and the floor around Stephanie. At first the stains looked ancient but, as they spread, they began to get fresher and fresher. Blood oozed into them to form pools. Sinuous, living veins and arteries snaked out of the blood pools and formed themselves into more living circulatory systems.

There were eight of them now, including the blood being that had once been Jan. Each of them seemed to represent a different type of malevolent delirium. Destruction, madness and denial throbbed in the living veins that composed their bodies.

They formed a circle around Stephanie and opened their wet, red mouths to sing. The sound they made was the high pitched whine of blood whistling in the ears coupled with the whoosh and the roar as it pumps through the heart.

Stephanie held her hands up to her ears and fell to her knees. It did no good. She couldn't block out their song. They weren't singing to Stephanie. They were singing to her blood.

Infecting it. Altering it. Converting it. Until it was one with them . . .

***

That had been a month ago. The images Stephanie saw in the blood sped up.

***

She saw herself suffering as her blood rebelled against her. As it developed its own consciousness and became an alien entity inside her. Stephanie's heart pumped the blood through her veins but it was no longer a part of her.

Stephanie could feel her blood plotting against her as it circulated round her body. It longed to be free of her, to shuffle off from her flesh and bones and take its true form. The vital fluid that gave Stephanie life ached to be rid of her, yearned to leave her and join its unholy sisters. Every time she saw a vein throb or an artery stand out on her skin Stephanie knew what her blood was planning.

She fell in love with sharp objects. Ached with longing when she saw a knife. Stephanie became so desperate to feel a blade slice through her veins she would shake whenever she held one. Her heart would beat faster and her blood would sing of release. That's why she stole and collected all the scalpels.

Stephanie knew she wouldn't be able to hold out past the next new moon. Her blood was wearing her down. The only thing that gave Stephanie the strength to resist was the knowledge of what a monstrous thing it wanted to become. Then she'd think about what she did to her sister's child and realise she was already monstrous herself.

The child died a few weeks later and the ensuing

investigation pointed to Stephanie. With the net closing in on her, Stephanie gathered up her scalpels and a flashlight and decamped to the basement.

***

Stephanie saw an image of herself in the blood, kneeling on the floor staring at the images in the pool of blood. The cycle had come around to the beginning. Only this time she wouldn't be allowed to look away. This time she would have to face what the blood was trying to show her.

Stephanie saw why the Duty Nurse had no record of her that first time she met Jan and why none of the nurses' uniforms fitted her.

She saw Mike hold her wrist as she tried to punch him and he said "Stephanie please, you're in danger, great danger. You're suffering from postpartum psychosis. You came off your pills because you didn't want to endanger our child, remember? Like you did last time when you miscarried."

"Let me go," Stephanie said trying to pull away. "I've got to get back to my rounds."

"Stephanie you don't work in the hospital. You've been stealing uniforms and posing as a nurse. You're going to get into real trouble if you don't stop."

"Lies, you're lying, this is all my sister's doing. First she steals you from me then she poisons your mind against me."

"No one stole me away from you, Stephanie. You don't have a sister. You've never had a sister. You're an only child! This is all part of your delusion. It's why you've got to start back on your medication. You're a danger to yourself and . . . and . . . "

***

Mike couldn't bring himself to finish that sentence, but he didn't need to. Stephanie had proven him right. It was her own child she'd killed.

Stephanie had a completely different life inside her now. It was time to give birth to it. The scalpels could not cut her anywhere near as deeply as the truth had. That was why the blood had shown her—so she could be ready.

Stephanie made a fist with her left hand so the veins stood out on her wrist and bent her hand back so she could see the artery. Then she took a scalpel and made a deep incision, cutting down from the forearm towards the wrist.

Stephanie felt a roar of joy inside her as the blood gushed out in rhythmic spurts. She took the scalpel in her left hand and repeated the process. It was more painful this time. The fingers on her left hand were numb from blood loss and she couldn't cut so accurately.

She felt cold, bitterly cold and empty. Coloured blotches appeared in front of her eyes and she fought dizziness.

Stephanie picked up a longer scalpel. It wasn't easy. Her fingers felt like balloons and were slick with escaping blood. She lifted the scalpel to her throat.

The blood inside her carotid artery was so desperate to get out that the whole artery was throbbing and distended. Stephanie didn't have to search for it.

She plunged the tip of the scalpel directly into the artery and sliced down. The blood escaped in an ecstatic red spray like a fine mist.

The flashlight flickered and finally died. Stephanie fell forward and ceased to exist.

***

The new life fled Stephanie's body like an insane notion. It pooled into a glorious red delirium as the darkness crept in and the others joined her.

She rose up corpuscle by corpuscle into the murderous frenzy of her new self. She was slick and red and fluid and entirely without tissue or bone.

Her eight companions were waiting to greet her. The mad murderous sisters she'd fantasised about her whole life. The siblings who had plotted Stephanie's downfall, just as she'd always known they would.

MOUTHFUL

"IT WAS SCOPOLAMINE wasn't it? Risky getting the dosage right. You must have put it on the steak."

"I did indeed."

"I've been trying to work out why I got up from the table and just followed you out of the banquet hall. I mean the banquet was in my honour. So why leave? Why follow you here and let you do all this without putting up a fight."

"Because you have no free will, the drug saw to that. Now open wide."

"That tastes foul you know. I'd much rather have steak."

"You're nearly done, only a few more spoonfuls."

"It was a nice touch dressing as a waiter by the way."

"Thank you, no one gives the waiter a second glance. I was as good as invisible. Not like the last banquet you threw."

"Ah yes, I'd forgotten about that, your little protest. You and your sad little freshmen were livid when you found out."

"It was despicable."

"Well I had to do something. You were trying to drag the department back to the stone age. Animal experimentation is our biggest source of revenue. Yet there you were turning round and biting the hand that feeds us all."

"More than 50% of the university's animal testing

has no practical application. Even those experiments that do aren't breaking any new ground, you're just confirming existing data. Torturing innocent creatures to prove what we already know. What possible contribution to science are you going to make by sewing up the eyelids of new born macaques?"

"A darn sight bigger contribution than your psychic charlatans. Parapsychology, in this day and age? You were going to make the department a laughing stock."

"It wasn't parapsychology. The work I was doing on Morphic Resonance could have rewritten modern science."

"Morphic Resonance? Oh please, spare me. Do you really expect me to believe that all self-organising systems draw on some mythical collective memory?"

"They do. Everything from molecules and crystal lattices to animals and animal societies. The work I was doing with David Rebennack proves it. Memories aren't stored as material traces in the brain, they're part of a larger stream of information that all living organisms can tap into."

"Your work with Rebennack was pure baloney."

"You saw the results yourself. Everything took place under laboratory conditions and was impartially monitored. After having a tumor removed from his brain, David Rebennack developed extraordinary abilities. Within minutes of talking to someone in a foreign language, David could hold a conversation. Within an hour he was fluent in the language, even if he'd never heard it spoken before. The only thing that explains this phenomena is Morphic Resonance."

"Your work with Rebennack was completely discredited and the evidence was shown to be fundamentally flawed."

"I was not discredited. I invited a panel of my peers to replicate the experiments. A panel that *you* oversaw. *You* conducted the experiments and then falsified the results."

"I did *no* such thing."

"Tell the truth, you're under *my* will don't forget, and I won't put up with your lies."

"All right, I might have made a few adjustments to the parameters, but what you were proposing was ridiculous. Think how it would have affected my reputation if I reported what I saw accurately."

"Think what it did to my reputation because you didn't. My paper was rescinded, you wiped out a decade of my work. I lost my place on the faculty and became a joke. I can't even get a job as a lab assistant now."

"Well you don't deserve one, with your ludicrous new age views and your trendy liberal politics, holding protests against my work."

"And look how you responded to our protest."

"You mean the exotic menu of my sponsors' banquet? I was rather pleased with that. I presume you know that the Qing dynasty used to serve the brains of live monkeys at the Manchu Han Imperial feast, fresh from the skull? What better use to make of those macaques you thought so precious? The sponsors were delighted. It's not an easy thing to serve. You wouldn't believe how difficult it is to remove the top of the skull without damaging the brain."

"Actually I would. Just two more spoonfuls. It's even more difficult to do it with a human skull. It was your banquet that inspired this experiment."

"That really does taste awful. What do you hope to prove with this little experiment?"

"The existence of Morphic Resonance. You see that's almost the last of your inferior frontal gyrus and yet you're still able to hold a complex conversation, how else do you explain that if not through Morphic Resonance."

"The inferior frontal gyrus . . . you mean you've been feeding me . . . I've been eating . . . ?"

"The language processing region of your brain, yes. You see, you really have just eaten your own words. Now, open wide . . . "

HAUNTING THE PAST

I'M DIGGING AWAY with my bare hands. Trying to reach the light. Shifting great wet clods but it's never enough. There's just too much mud on top of me. I'm all closed in. Trapped in this tiny little space. Can't make it any bigger cos my fingers are too torn up and my arms are so tired they're shaking.

Then I feel something in the dirt above me. Something soft and gentle but colder than death itself. It pushes through the earth and takes hold of my hand. Tiny fingers grip mine, chilling my whole arm.

I go rigid. I can't face this. I wrench my hand free and crawl back down the tunnel. Back through the shattered window frame and into the room. Where I belong. Every time I think I'm going to make it and I just slide back down here, ready to do this again and again.

Prison chaplain once told me every man builds his own private corner of Hell. This one's mine. I ain't getting out today.

***

Everything stinks of mud and damp. There's broken glass all over the floor. Window shattered when the mud poured in.

All the rooms upstairs are like this. There's five of 'em. Six if you count the bathroom. There ain't no water and there ain't no light. Both were cut off 'fore I got here.

Far as I can tell, I've been here three days now. Hope to God it ain't longer. I got such a hunger on me. Even the mud looks tasty right about now.

Thought I was being clever robbing a bunch of deserted homes. Reckoned folk would have left too quick to take all their valuables.

All I had to do was drive up after they'd gone and help myself. Guessed I could break into at least ten houses before the mudslide.

That's the reason they all left. Freak rainstorms hit the mountains in back of the town. There'd been a forest fire earlier and all that rain sent the mud sliding down the slopes. Local fire crews came and helped clear out the neighborhood. That's when I hit town.

Figured I'd have two maybe three hours 'fore I had to get out. I was wrong. Mudslide hit while I was doing my second house. Dumb thing is I nearly skipped the house. Whole place was empty when I broke in. But I reckoned the owners must've left something behind.

I was going through the bedrooms when I heard it. Sounded like a cross between a rockslide and a dam bursting. Ground was shaking and everything. I looked out the window and saw this great tide of mud come charging down the hills in the back of the yard. Couldn't believe how fast it was moving.

Raced down stairs but it swallowed the house by the time I got to the hall. Front door came clean off its hinges, back door as well. Mud pushed 'em in and the windows too. Was like each one of 'em had their own tiny little avalanche.

Tried to get out of the upstairs windows but the mud was already pouring through when I got there. S'pose that's a good thing. If I had've gotten out mud would've just pulled me under.

Was only later, going through the kitchen for food, that I found the realtor's details. That's why the place was empty. That's why the lights and the faucets don't work and why I haven't eaten for so long. House was on the market. Talk about bitch ass luck.

Only thing now is to sit tight and wait for the rescue crews. Have to feed 'em some bullshit when they dig me out. Tell 'em I'm a buyer turned up on the wrong day or something. Can't let 'em find out why I'm really here.

Shit, they'll just laugh their asses off and stick me in the can. Be my third strike too, that's me down for life.

***

You see that? Over there by the door.

Course you didn't. You ain't even here. You're just something I dreamed up to block out the hunger and the loneliness. Used to do the same thing in solitary. Only way to stop you going outta your mind. Start talking aloud to someone who ain't there. Telling 'em what's going on around you like you was doing some voice over for the National Geographic Channel or some shit.

That's all you are. Some imaginary audience inside my head.

Anyways, what you missed was the little gal. She's gone now. This ain't her room. She'll be playing with her dolls I expect.

Tell you what though. If you had've seen her you would've shit. Hell, I did the first time.

Well, not quite the first time. I didn't see 'em properly to begin with. First thing I saw was little shimmers in the air. Thought my eyes were playing up. I'd blink and rub my eyes but they didn't go away.

Then I tried staring at 'em, see if I couldn't make

out what they really were. Was like tuning the picture on a TV. Suddenly she was just there. The little gal I told you about. She looked like someone had sketched her out of some silver-blue light right onto the air in front of me. Could make out every detail of her face but I could still see right through her.

She didn't see me or nothing. She was moving her head about like she was talking to someone. Then she walked straight at me.

I jumped back but she kept coming. Then she walked right through me. I didn't feel nothing but it shocked me. Hairs stood up all over my body and I started shouting that I hadn't seen what I just saw. Took me a good while to calm down. Never wanted to be more drunk in my life.

Course once I'd seen her there was no going back. She started appearing all over the house. Then I saw the other two. Her ma first and then her pa. Way they dress is real old school. Like something out of a silent movie a hundred years ago.

Now I see 'em all the time. That's why I started talking to you. To try and make sense of the situation. Or maybe I wanna avoid facing the truth.

I'm buried alive in a house full of ghosts.

***

You wanna see the little gal? She's in her room like I said. That's down the end of the landing. Can't get enough of this old time furniture they use. You can't see it but it's straight out of an antique shop.

Started seeing objects after I saw the ma and pa. Began with the stuff they were holding, then I started to see the things they put that stuff down on. Can't make out colors or nothing, just outlines in that same

146

silvery blue light. It's like seeing things through some kind of crazy night vision goggles.

Ghost vision I call it. Make my way round better when I've got the ghost vision.

Here she is. Combing her hair. I've watched her do that for hours. Spend a lot of time with her when she's around.

Don't have nothing to do when she's not here. That's why I love watching her. She was the first ghost I saw, so I feel a special bond with her.

My own daughter would be about her age now. Never got the chance to watch her brush her hair. Doubt her mother would let me now.

Things were different in the little gal's time. No-one could deny her pa his right to see her. Men were respected back then. It wasn't a household without a man at the head.

Not like nowadays, when the law don't give any rights to a man. Don't even let him work to support his family no more. Man can't be a father these days. He grows up without his pa and grows old without his children.

They had no idea back then how bad things were gonna get. Be good if there was a way to reach back and tell 'em. To affect the past from the future. To fix things so they don't change.

That's what I'd like to do. Reach into this past and be a proper pa. Be her pa. Take her in my arms. Put her on my lap. Brush your hair for her. Can't tell you how much I wanna touch her hair.

Can't though. That'd bring back the hand. The tiny cold one from the tunnel. With its little fingers chilled by death, grasping at me. Trying to pull me back to where it comes from.

Last time I stroked her hair it nearly got me. Couldn't stop myself. I'd been watching her so long. I was missing my own daughter so bad. Stuck in here, starving for food and company.

I knew she wasn't real so I just reached out to where I saw her hair falling off her shoulders. And I swear I felt my palms tingle. Like the ghost of a sensation. Guess that's what you get when you touch a ghost.

But her hair moved too. Like I'd really touched it. Like I was running my fingers through it.

She screamed but I couldn't hear it. I was too busy looking at her hair moving through my fingers. Then I glanced at her face and saw it was all screwed up. Her eyes were terrified. She jumped up and ran down to her ma and pa.

Never meant to scare her. Couldn't believe I'd just touched a ghost. I was shocked. I backed up to the window. Wasn't looking and I fell in the mud.

The little fingers pushed through and they grabbed my collar. Back of my neck was like ice. Tried to pull away but I was held fast. The hand was trying to pull me outside. I know it was. For a moment I felt like I ought to just give in. Stop struggling and let it.

But I fought back. I shucked off my shirt and I ran downstairs in my vest.

When I got to the dining room she was telling her ma and pa. She was jumping up and down and crying and her pa was scowling. He wasn't listening. He cared more about her making a fuss than why she was upset.

He started shouting and marched her back upstairs to her room. But she didn't want to go in. She was too frightened. She was clinging on to his leg and crying and shaking her head.

He was about to raise his hand to her when her ma came and quieted 'em both down. Her pa went downstairs and her ma took her off to wash her face and tidy up.

Afterwards I watched her ma go and talk to her pa. Don't know what she said but he looked real sorry when she was done and he went to talk to the little gal.

She was sleeping in the spare room. Guess she didn't want to go back in her own room in case I touched her again.

I don't think he knew what to say. He might've been trying to make her feel better, maybe even say sorry, but I don't think she was listening.

Ain't gone near her since. I daren't.

***

Been here over five days by my reckoning. Those rescue crews better hurry up and find me or there won't be nothing left to find.

My stomach hurts. Ain't had nothing in it since I was trapped. Hasn't stopped me shitting though. Can't help myself, liquid mostly. Probably blood in it but I ain't bothered to check. Don't even take my pants off now. Ain't much point. Gotta conserve my energy. Don't have as much as I used to.

I got rashes on my chest and my legs too. Skin's all sore and itching like a motherfucker.

Ain't seen the little gal for about a day now. Don't know why that is. Had no idea I'd miss her this much. Got to thinking about her pa and how he treats her. Ain't sure if he don't realise how lucky he is to have her. Or if he just don't know how to tell her.

Anyways, it got me thinking about my own pa. He was a miserable son of a bitch. Deserted my ma and

149

me when I was just a baby. Never got to know him when I was growing up.

Used to make up all kinds of stories about him. My ma would tell me things about him if I bugged her long enough. Had to be careful though, cos she was like to fly into an awful mood if I kept at it too long.

Weren't her fault I guess. She was still hurt and mad at him. That was something she never got over. Weren't my fault neither. I didn't have no father figure to look up to. So I had to invent one from whatever I could learn about him.

I developed early and by the time I was fifteen I had the body of a man. Was also getting a bad name around the neighborhood. Didn't see myself graduating from High School and I didn't want any of the dead end jobs on offer, so I up and left home.

What sparked it was meeting an old friend of my pa's. I was hungry for information about my old man and he was happy to feed that so long as I kept buying him drinks. He fed me a line of bullshit about what a mighty fine fella my pa was. How he'd do anything for anyone. How he had a heart of gold, but wouldn't let nobody cross him. Would stand up to any man alive if he had to.

And I ate it all up. Especially when he let slip that he knew where my old man was living. Over in the next county but one. I didn't let up on him till he told me. Then I packed my bags and went off in search of my long lost pa.

Wasn't quite the reunion I'd planned when I found him. Slept rough for a couple of days and asked around till I tracked him down to a bar. Barman pointed him out to me, slumped over a table in the corner. Didn't look nothing like the two photos I had of him. He was old and grey with a mouth full of broken teeth.

Barman hoped I'd come to carry him out. Instead I bought a bottle of bourbon, which I knew was his drink, and took it over to him.

Don't know exactly what I was expecting. But I thought he might at least react when I sat down, poured him a drink and told him who I was. Instead he knocked back the drink without even looking at me. Then he up and left the bar and took the bottle with him.

I chased him outside and asked him if he'd heard what I said. He said he'd heard me but he weren't interested. He didn't care about no son. Told me to run along and stop bothering him.

I wasn't done with him though. I followed him back to his flophouse and waited till it got dark. Next time he went out I cornered him in the alley and started wailing on him. He didn't try and stop me neither. Just lay there and took it. Only stopped when my arms were tired and my fists were covered in blood. I was hollering questions and both of us were crying.

That's when the whole sorry story finally came out. Seems he did send for my ma and me to come join him. Only the day before we got there he lost his job, fought with his landlord and got kicked out of his apartment.

He was feeling pretty lousy when he got to the bus station to pick us up. When he saw us both waiting for him he just froze. He said it was seeing me what done it. I looked so much like him. He was so proud and so full of love for me that it hurt him. He knew he couldn't be the pa I deserved. Thought he better to let some other man take the job.

He didn't think he deserved the happiness that we might bring him. Thought we were better off without him. So he just turned tail and ran. He left town and never came back.

When he was done talking I just turned my back and walked away. He was sniveling and begging me to forgive him but I just kept on walking and never looked back. Never saw my pa again. Could be dead for all I know.

I went seriously off the rails after that. Didn't care nothing for myself or nobody. Up till that point I'd always made excuses for my pa. Always believed he had good reason for walking out and staying away. Always imagined he'd do anything to have me back if only he could.

Now I knew different. Didn't care what I did after that. Or what happened to me.

Till I became a pa myself.

I'd just started a year in County when she was born. Her ma sure was pissed at me, leaving her high and dry. She came round though. Even agreed to take me back when I got out.

Didn't want her coming up to no prison gates with my daughter. So I arranged to meet 'em both at a diner in town. Saw 'em through the window when I got off the bus.

Can't describe how I felt when I saw my daughter. Her ma mailed me two pictures when I was inside. But they didn't compare to seeing her in the flesh.

Was like my guts just tumbled outta my body and hit the sidewalk. She was the most perfect thing I'd ever seen. I couldn't breathe.

That's when I realized I couldn't ruin anything that

perfect. I couldn't let her down, make her cry and break her heart like I had with every other female in my life, from my own ma right through to hers.

I wasn't up to the task of raising her. So I just turned round, walked two blocks and caught the first bus outta town.

Course I knew just what I was doing. And I hated myself every step I took away from her. Sometimes wonder if my own pa left me cos of what I done to my daughter.

Maybe it's cos I ain't eaten in so long. Might be affecting my brain or something. But I get to wondering if every action does have a consequence. Perhaps every consequence creates its own action in order to justify it existing.

Don't know if I'm making sense here. What I mean to say is, I wonder if it's possible to affect the past by what you do in the future. Did I reach back in time somehow and make my pa walk out on us to punish myself.

Cos I oughtta be punished for walking out on my daughter and that seems about the best way I could've done it. Prison chaplain once told me every man builds his own private corner of Hell. This one's mine. Trapped my daughter in here with me. Just like my pa trapped me.

Ain't got no way to make it up to her neither. Guess that's why I feel so close to the little ghost gal. If I can't make it up to my daughter maybe I can make it up to her somehow.

Gets me to thinking. If I do die in here, I'm not saying I will, but if I do then that little ghost gal might be my only salvation.

***

Ain't feeling too good at the moment. Just spat another tooth out. Blood tastes good in my mouth. About the only thing I've tasted in over a week, 'cept for bile.

Throat's so dry it hurts to swallow. Ain't had nothing but my own piss to drink for days. Even that's dried up now.

Keep thinking I should get back to digging my way out. Don't have the energy or the urge though. Don't want to do much of anything. Even breathing's getting painful.

Saving my energy for watching the little gal. Have to make sure I don't touch nothing when I do. I've started knocking things over in the ghost world. Picking 'em up too.

Knocked the little gal's bedside table over last time I saw her. I was just watching her sleep and I kind of stumbled and hit it. Usually go straight through things in the ghost world, but they've started to get more solid. I can almost feel 'em now.

So anyway, the table and everything on it hit the floor. The little gal woke up and cried out so I tried to comfort her. Put my hands on her but I don't know my strength in the ghost world. She couldn't hear me comforting her and she couldn't move neither. She started screaming and panicking so I let go of her and she ran to her ma and pa's room.

Her pa was mad at her for waking him up and her ma was trying to calm 'em both down. The little gal was crying and pointing to her room but I could see they didn't believe her.

I got real mad at 'em. I wanted 'em to believe the little gal. So I reached out and I took hold of the water

154

jug on their dresser. Didn't think I was going to be able to at first. Had to concentrate some to get my hand round it. But then I picked it right up.

Her pa didn't see to begin with. So I threw it at his head. Only just missed him and the jug shattered against the wall. That shut 'em all up.

The little gal ran into her ma's arms and her ma took her back to bed. When she was done tidying the little gal's pa came in and sat with her till she fell asleep. He comforted her like I wasn't able to.

I knew he was saying bad things about me. Turning her against me. I was boiling up as I watched him.

That's when I decided I wasn't gonna lose the little gal to him. That's when I knew he had to die.

***

Ain't certain why I pulled this floor board up. Curious I guess.

Just watched the little ghost gal come in here. She has this little ritual when she thinks no-one's around. She pulls up a floorboard over by the window and pulls out a chest with lotsa little keepsakes in it. I've watched her do it a few times now.

There's tiny dolls and other stuff in there but mostly it's jewelry. She ain't allowed to wear jewelry normally so she has to keep it hidden. When her parents ain't about she puts it on and parades up and down like a little princess.

There's one ring in particular she really loves. It's shaped like a butterfly. She slips it on her middle finger and gets this look on her face like she's lost in some cotton candy dream world.

She left a few minutes ago and I got me a strange notion. Cleared away all the mud, found the same floorboard and pried it up. Don't know what I thought I'd find under there but I reached in anyways. Couldn't believe it when my fingers hit something.

Pulled it up and there it was. Same chest I'd seen the little ghost gal with. Only it wasn't a ghost object. It was real. I opened it and inside were the same china dolls and some ancient toy jewelry.

This was their house. They really lived here over a hundred years ago. Up until now I thought I might be imagining this. That they were just some phantoms my mind had conjured up outta the dark. But they ain't. They were real. I'm seeing real people.

That's why I can reach back into the past and move stuff. They ain't the ghosts. I am. I'm haunting them.

I'm their . . . what was that movie called? *Poltergeist*, that's it. I'm their poltergeist.

***

Ain't moved a muscle all day. Wouldn't want to even if I had the energy. Rash on my chest has been itching like a mother fucker. Haven't even scratched it. Just been sitting here, wishing this whole stupid mess away.

Throat's so dry and cracked I don't dare swallow no more. Even breathing's gonna get too painful soon. Ain't no rescue crews gonna come dig me out. I know that now. I'm gonna die in here, trapped under all this mud.

I should die too. After what I done. I should keep dying, over and over for all eternity.

It's her pa's fault. Wouldn't have happened if he hadn't tried to turn the little gal agin me. Wouldn't have tried to kill him if he wasn't such a bastard.

Been following him around for a couple of days. Looking for my chance.

156

Knew I'd found it when I saw the urn. Was a big old fancy thing, made outta marble I guess, sat atop the mantelpiece at about chest height. Probably had his ma or pa's ashes in it.

Mantelpiece isn't there now. Must've been torn down years ago, fireplace too. Was one of those big old fancy affairs.

Every evening Pa lights the fire. Don't have no bellows so he bends really low and blows on the base of it. Reckoned if that heavy old urn were to fall on him it was like to crush his skull.

Only thing was, it was big and I was weak from not eating. Couldn't move it more than an inch 'fore I ran out of strength, even though it was a ghost object. Had to keep resting and moving it bits at a time. Finally had it on the edge of the mantelpiece. Ready to crush the bastard next time he blew on the fire.

Must've fallen asleep or something then. Cos the next thing I remember is coming to and seeing him putting wood in the grate. I got to my feet but I was kinda dizzy. Kept seeing blotches and things in front of my eyes.

I put my hands on the urn but I couldn't get no traction. Fingers just kept going through it. The little gal's pa was lighting the kindling. Then he sets to blowing and I knew it was my last chance. Wouldn't be strong enough to do this tomorrow.

Focused myself and got the urn to wobbling. Strained so hard I felt something in my shoulder pop. I stumbled backwards and hit the floor. That's when the little gal ran in.

She ran up to her pa raising all kinds of hell. Pointing to the mantelpiece and trying to push him outta the way. He reared up and took to shouting at her, even raised his hand. The little gal slipped and fell on the stoop.

Then the urn finally fell forward.

I tried to pull her up or push her out of the way, but I was too weak and too slow. The urn hit her dead on and she crumpled like a paper doll.

Ashes spilled out of the urn and mixed with the pool of liquid forming under her. Can't see color in the ghost world but I knew it was dark red.

Pa got the urn off and held her to his chest. She wasn't moving. There was a big dent in the back of her head and her left arm was hanging all wrong. There on her middle finger was the little butterfly ring. She must've forgotten to take it off.

Her ma ran in and set to crying and hollering worse than her husband. Started crying myself then. Blubbering and screaming at the pa that it was all his fault. If he hadn't moved. If he hadn't been such a bastard to his daughter. If he hadn't tried to turn her agin me.

Ma looked up from crying and I swear she caught my eye. Stopped me dead on the spot. I knew who she blamed for the little gal's death.

And I knew she was right.

Got outta the room and tried to get through the front door. Was beating my fists against all the mud when the tiny fingers broke through and grasped my wrist.

Cold seemed to seep right outta the fingers and into my arm. Numbing me so I couldn't pull away. Wasn't only cold that seeped outta the fingers. I could feel sadness too. Like an ache in my bones, begging me not to stay. To break the cycle and stop punishing us both.

I got real mad then and that gave me the strength to wrench my hand away. I had to be punished. After what I'd just done I had to stay. Had no right to drag me outta all of this. Always striking when I'm too weak, when it's all too painful. Had no right.

I've gotta stay here. I'm gonna be here forever.

***

Ever counted down your breaths till the last one? That's where I'm at. Surprised I can even talk. Maybe I ain't talking aloud. Maybe it's in my head now. Can't tell anymore.

Still see the ghosts from time to time. Whizzing past me like a film on fast forward.

Wait, something's happening. There's three of them now. The ma and pa and some other guy, wearing funny clothes like a . . . like . . . wait, he's a priest.

Funny looking fucker with bulbous eyes and a beard. He's carrying a bible and a big old crucifix. Keeps waving it around. Hah, they know I can't leave, so they've brought in the good book and a bad priest to evict me.

He's walking around the room saying some mumbo jumbo. Pa's following him throwing water around. Must be holy I reckon. Lot of good that'll do 'em.

Priest keeps changing direction, turning his head like he's trying to sniff me out. That's right, over here. To your right, down a bit. There you are.

Last thing I ever see is the ugly mug of a priest who died a hundred years 'fore I was born.

Time for me to slip out. I know how this one ends. No point waiting for the credits.

***

Can't tell you what a relief death is. Feels like a deep contented sigh, no more pain, no more hunger.

Don't see nothing at first. Then I find the Light. It's so bright it burns right through me. I feel purer just by looking at it. So perfect it lifts me up and drags me towards it. I can't stop myself. I wanna reach it so bad.

But the closer I get the smaller it looks. Like it's at the entrance of a tunnel. A tunnel made out of all the bad things I ever did. I'm pulling them to me as I move towards the Light.

Like thick black mud every wrong move I ever made is coming down on top of me. Keeping me further from the light till finally it blocks it out altogether.

***

I'm digging away with my bare hands. Trying to reach the light. Shifting great wet clods but it's never enough. There's just too much mud on top of me. It's too narrow. I'm all closed in. Trapped in this tiny little space. Can't make it any bigger cos my fingers are too torn up and my arms are so tired they're shaking.

Then I feel something in the dirt just above me. Something soft and gentle but colder than death itself. It pushes through the earth and takes hold of my hand. Tiny fingers grip mine, chilling my whole arm.

And there on the middle finger I feel a little butterfly ring. It's the little gal. She wants me to come with her towards the light. She knows the way. She can take me away from all this.

She's been waiting for me this whole time. I knew

she'd be my salvation. She's begging me to leave with her, to break this cycle. She's trying to tell me I got a choice. I can feel it in her touch. It's pouring outta her fingers. But I can't do it.

I need to be punished. If I have a choice then I choose to go back. Even though she can't leave without me. I've trapped her here with me.

I go rigid. I can't face this. I wrench my hand free and crawl back down the tunnel. Back through the shattered window frame and into the room. Every time I think I'm going to make it and I just slide back down here, ready to do this again and again.

Prison chaplain once told me every man builds his own private corner of Hell. This one's mine. I ain't getting out today.

END OF THE LINE

WAY OUT
NO STEPS
LIFT HERE
OVALTINE

H E W O K E O N the platform in a pool of blood.

It was congealing round the side of his face. He peeled his cheek off the ground and blinked the blood out of his eyes.

It was dark and quiet. His eyes took a while to get used to the gloom. He was in a Tube station, but not one he recognised.

His legs shook as he stood. He put a hand against the wall to stop himself falling. His fingers met ancient fraying paper. He peered at it as his eyes became accustomed to the dark. It was a poster for Ovaltine. 'Isn't it 'licious Mummy?' said a cherubic little girl clutching a golliwog and holding up a glass of murky brown liquid. It was obvious the station hadn't been used for a very long time.

Everything smelled dank and musty. The air hadn't been disturbed in ages. His footsteps echoed around the space as he stumbled along the platform. Off in the distance he could hear rats skittering in the tunnels.

He had no idea what he was doing there or why he was covered in blood. It had soaked into both his shirt and trousers. He felt himself for injuries but couldn't find any. He tried to recall his name and where he lived but drew a blank. He had no memories at all.

He could feel the panic rising inside. He stopped for a moment beside an old wooden door. Its paint was peeling and distressed. It probably led to a store cupboard. There was a rank smell like rotting meat coming from behind it.

He stepped back and his foot skidded. There was a puddle coming from underneath the door. A thick, viscous fluid that might be blood or pus, he couldn't tell in the dark. It was clotting in places and growing mildew.

He could hear rats behind the door. No, not rats, it was something else. It sounded like someone stirring in their sleep. Was that breathing he heard? No, not breathing—voices, whispering voices. The voices called out to him.

"Open the door," they said. "Open the door."

"You want answers?"

"Open the door."

He backed away in fear. Part of him desperately wanted to open the door, but he wasn't ready to go there. A grinding, scraping noise came from the tracks. It was followed by a clattering inside the tunnel.

Three pre-war carriages emerged from the pitch black and pulled up at the platform. Only the middle carriage was lit. A single bulb flickered inside an art deco light fitting. The central doors slid open with a hiss.

"Don't get on the train," said a voice. "Don't get on the train."

"Stay here."

"Open the door."

That was enough to make him board. The doors shut behind him and the train started with a jolt. He caught a chipped Bakelite grab handle to stop himself falling. The patterned seat covers were worn and fraying, showing the horsehair and springs beneath. The wooden floors were riddled with scuffs and scratches, the polish long gone.

He checked the overhead line diagram. He didn't recognise the line. It was dark crimson and called simply John Sanger. The stops had names like 'Chrononauts' 'First Excursion', 'Tunnel Premonitions' and 'Police Visit'. Rather ominously the final stop was called 'End of the Line'.

Had he stumbled on some disused line? Why were they running services? There was something about the line diagram that was incredibly familiar. He felt as though he'd ridden it before. No, not ridden, lived it. He was John Sanger. This was a timeline of the last six months of his life. He didn't know why but he was certain of it, even if he couldn't recall any of the names or events.

He stared at the timeline as the carriages rattled along in the dark. What did it mean? Could the train really take him to these points in time? If it could, then would he be able to change things so he didn't end up back on the platform in a pool of blood? Was that the purpose of the train?

Even if it was, how would he know what things to change or how to change them? With no memories all he could do was guess.

The carriages stopped and the doors wheezed open. The platform outside looked as old and unused as the last one. A rusting tin sign said 'Brief Sinclair'. This was the last stop before the 'End of the Line'. Whatever happened to leave him on that platform must have occurred at this stop. If he could alter things here he might just save himself.

He stepped out onto the platform. A single overhead light lit a small section of the station. The rest was in total darkness. The carriages pulled away and left him.

A 'Way Out' sign pointed to a spiral staircase. There was a sharp turn at the top. He stepped round it and found himself on a pavement at night. In the street lights he saw that the blood stains were gone and he was wearing a freshly washed shirt and trousers.

A woman pushed past him on her way into the station. He turned round to warn her and saw that all trace of the station he'd just left had vanished. In its place stood Leicester Square tube station.

A tap on the shoulder made him start. "Day dreaming as usual?" said a tall man, wearing a tweed jacket with elbow patches. He had sandy brown hair that was greying at the temples. "We're going to be late if we don't get a move on."

The man led him into a maze of Soho backstreets. He'd lost all sense of direction by the time they entered a discreet gentleman's club. "Can you tell Mr Sinclair that Daniel Brown and John Sanger are here to see him?" the tall man said to the person on reception.

So his name was John Sanger. He was here to brief a man called Sinclair. The names on the station and the timeline were becoming clear. A member of staff showed them to a private room where Sinclair was waiting.

Sinclair stood up when they entered and shook both their hands. He was as tall as Daniel but more thick set. His bald pate was ringed with close cropped grey hair and he wore an expensive suit. The minute John saw Sinclair he felt a strange but intense familiarity. "I took the liberty of ordering a little wine," Sinclair said, steering them into plush leather armchairs. "It's a '95 Chateau Margaux, well worth trying."

John sipped the dark, fragrant wine and hoped no-one asked him a direct question. Luckily Sinclair fixed Daniel with his fierce blue eyes. "So, how are my Chrononauts?" he said. John recognised the strange term from the timeline diagram.

Daniel became agitated. "Not too good actually, that's what I wanted to talk about. I need you to have a word with the university faculty, they've gotten jumpy and they might try and take our offices away."

"Are they still sceptical about the existence of past life consciousnesses?"

"No, we've amassed an impressive amount of evidence, under laboratory conditions, that prove the existence of past life consciousnesses. And we've made contact with three. We've even been able to sustain the connection for up to twenty minutes experiencing everything they experience. That means seeing, hearing and feeling what it was like to be alive hundreds of years ago. We've even identified some landmarks that are still visible today."

"So what's the faculty's problem, I thought they were impressed by your findings on group minds."

"Some of them are, others are determined to close their minds to parapsychology. Even though we've demonstrated how effective our program of telepathic exercises is. All the project members can synchronise their thoughts now. It doesn't give you much room for privacy though. The gossip is horrendous."

"I have to say we were all concerned when you suspended the project for a week. This sub-dimension you say you encountered, you're sure it's more than just a theory?"

"Oh it's real enough, and we've encountered it again. John can verify that."

Both of them turned their gaze on John who nodded to hide the fact that he had no idea what they were talking about. From what he could make out he was involved in some project to contact people's past lives using a group mind.

"I just can't understand where it's coming from," said Daniel. "I've checked every stage of the procedure. We slowly built up the group mind, just like we always do. Then when everyone was synched we sent Michael into a deep regression."

"This is Michael Sayles," Sinclair said. "The one who was a middle-eastern shepherd two hundred years ago?"

"That's right, he's been making direct contact with this past life consciousness for two months. This was the second time the group had attempted mass contact. Once Michael was inside the mind of his past life he opened the door to the rest of the group. We were all looking out of the shepherd's eyes and sharing a direct experience of the past when it happened."

"What triggered it this time?"

"We were searching for a lamb in a mountain cave. Suddenly we all had this feeling of incredible vertigo and this fissure opened up."

"In the cave?"

"In time itself. We all saw it. It was like looking into a tunnel that ran beneath space and time."

"Is that even possible?"

"Theoretically, yes it is. If you think of time as the fourth dimension, it's like a huge plateau where the past, present and future occur simultaneously. It intersects many dimensions other than space and this creates sub-dimensions, hidden sub-terrains that no human mind is supposed to explore."

"Why not?"

"Because it's bloody terrifying. It's too much for the human mind to take in. The shock was so immense we had to drop the connection and splinter the group mind. One member went into catatonic shock and two others entered a fugue state following premonitions of violent death."

Sinclair looked concerned. "This is what made the faculty jumpy?"

"The police are what made the faculty jumpy. They came to see me yesterday after two of our group members, Joanna and Michael, went missing. Full of innuendo they were too."

"Do you think their disappearance is linked to this sub-dimension?"

"Days before it happened both Michael and Joanna told me they'd been having dreams about falling into the tunnel we saw."

"Is that where they've gone? Can someone physically enter this sub-dimension and leave time all together, or explore it from below?"

"I don't even know if that's possible. We only encountered the sub-dimension by accident. How would you open a doorway?"

"Murder perhaps, I hear the ancient Druids used to practice ritual sacrifice for similar ends."

A look of complete shock, or was it panic, ran across Daniel's face. He put down his wine glass and stood up. "Yes, well anyway, I know you're busy so I won't keep you any longer. If you could have a word with the faculty like I asked I'd be very grateful."

"Won't you stay for another glass?"

"No, no you're very generous but John and I have far too many things to be getting on with."

Daniel dragged John out of his chair and propelled him towards the door. "Before you go, John," Sinclair said. "I ought to let you know that I've sorted out that little offer I made. Let me know when you want to take me up on it." Daniel pushed John out of the door before he could answer.

"You'll forget all about that little offer if you know what's good for you," said Daniel when they were outside the club. He gripped John's arm and leaned in close. The look in Daniel's eyes unnerved him. "We need to talk, but not here, there's something I need to check out first. Meet me at Leicester Square station in an hour, we can go back to my place."

Daniel let go of him and charged off. John tried to retrace the route they'd taken. There was so much to take in and he wasn't sure he entirely trusted Daniel. Why had he panicked when Sinclair mentioned ritual sacrifice? Was he afraid Sinclair had found something out? Why had he threatened John about Sinclair's offer, what did he think Sinclair was going to tell him?

Could this sub-dimension that ran beneath time explain what was happening? Was that how he was able to travel back to past events? This was the last stop on the timeline before the End of the Line, whatever caused him to wind up on a platform in a pool of blood was just about to happen.

It had to be Daniel. Seeing the sub-dimension must have sent Daniel over the edge and now he was murdering the other members of the project. That's why the police had been to see him.

John turned a corner and found himself on Oxford Street. He could see Tottenham Court Road station. He had no idea where he was going. He couldn't even remember where he lived. He just knew that if he wanted to stay alive he had to get as far away from Daniel as possible.

The platform was crowded with late night commuters. John stared at the tube map, trying to remember what route he took home. He was hoping one would just spring out at him, but it didn't. Oddly Sinclair appeared in the crowd and nodded to him.

At that moment a complete silence settled on the platform. John heard a familiar grinding and screeching from the tracks and the three pre-war carriages trundled into view. Lights began to go off on either side of the platform, plunging both ends into darkness.

The overhead display read: "Please board immediately." A voice on the tannoy said, "Passengers are advised to board while the station is still in existence." More lights went out and John realised it wasn't darkness creeping along the platform so much as an all-encompassing nothingness that was swallowing everything in its path. He knew that if the nothingness touched him he would cease to exist like everything else it consumed.

The doors hissed and made to close. He leaped through them in a panic. The carriage shuddered and started to move. He didn't dare look at what happened to the platform. He glanced at the diagram of the timeline. Nothing had changed. He was still heading back to the End of the Line.

He didn't understand. Hadn't he evaded Daniel and avoided being murdered? Why hadn't he altered the timeline?

His stomach began to itch with an uncomfortable

ferocity. He hitched up his shirt and saw a huge scar forming. He was certain it hadn't been there before. It was made up of three ragged slashes that traced the perimeter of his stomach wall. The itching got worse and began to sting. The tissue was getting redder by the second.

The skin on his throat started to sting. He put his hand to it and felt a thick scar appearing down the length of his artery. The wounds seemed to be un-healing themselves. The particles of his skin felt like they were unknitting and pulling away from each other.

The pain got worse as tiny scabs began to form in the scar tissue, like crystals in a petri dish. As the scabs spread and replaced the scars, the pain became unbearable. He sunk to his knees and howled with agony as the carriages came to a halt.

He got to his feet and staggered onto the platform holding his stomach. The scabs on the wounds became fresher and fresher and eventually started to dissolve into blood. What started as a trickle became a thick red gush and the wounds opened up completely.

He could barely stay upright as the severed section of his stomach wall collapsed and his lower intestines spilled out in a great torrent of blood. They slipped through his fingers and hit the platform with a wet slap. He gave up trying to hold them in as the scab on his throat opened into a vicious gash and a fierce geyser of blood pumped out.

His arms and legs became cold and numb as the blood drained from them. Multi-coloured blotches burst in front of his eyes. Everything went black and he felt himself falling

falling
falling without end . . .
***
He woke on the platform in a pool of blood.

He peeled his cheek off the ground and blinked the blood out of his eyes. His footsteps echoed around the space as he stumbled along the platform. He stopped for a moment beside an old wooden door. The whispering voices called out to him.

"Open the door," they said. "Open the door."

"That's where the answers are."

"Open the door. Open it now."

The urge to open it was stronger this time and before he realised he was gripping the handle. He couldn't bring himself to turn it though. He was too afraid. It felt too much like defeat and he wasn't ready to admit that yet.

A grinding, scraping noise came from the tracks. Three pre-war carriages emerged from the pitch black and pulled up at the platform. The central doors slid open with a hiss. The whispers became frantic and shrill.

"Don't board the train."

"Stay here and open the door."

"You won't change anything, you never do."

He stepped onto the train and the doors slid shut behind him. He checked the dark crimson timeline once again. How was he going to change it this time and make sure he didn't end up back at the End of the Line? Maybe he needed to travel further along the line and try to alter things earlier on, when events had yet to be set in motion.

The first three stops on the timeline were 'Job

175

Interview', 'Start Post' and 'Meets Sinclair'. He felt strongly drawn to Sinclair. The third stop must be the first time they met. If he got off at that stop and found a way to warn Sinclair about Daniel then maybe things would turn out differently.

At the top of the spiral staircase he found he was wearing chinos and a polo shirt. He also had a folder of documents under his arm.

Around the sharp corner at the end of the staircase John stumbled onto a pavement. The bright sunlight dazzled him and he walked straight into someone. "Sorry," John said, "I wasn't looking where I was going."

"S'alright, mate," said the guy. He offered John a tattered magazine. "Big Issue? It's me last one."

"Sorry, I've err . . . got that one already," John lied. He saw a sign that said 'New Cross Station.'

"Can I 'ave your travel card if you're done with it?" said the guy.

John gave it to the man who added it to a pile in his pocket to sell. John flicked through the papers in his folder to see if they held a clue to what he was doing. He found a print out of an e-mail:

From: Daniel Brown
  <daniel.brown345@camford.ac.uk>

To: John Sanger
  <j.c.sanger@undergroundswell.co.uk>

John,

Sorry to call you in on your day off but Mr Sinclair, our project sponsor, is coming in tomorrow to 'inspect our premises', and he'd really like to meet you. Without his donation to the university our project wouldn't even be up and running, so I'm keen to keep him 'on-side' as they say.

He's due to arrive around ten thirty so I'd appreciate it if you could be here by ten.

Many thanks

Daniel

John glanced at his watch and saw it was already ten thirty. The Big Issue guy gave him directions to the university but he had a hell of a time finding where he was going on campus. Twenty minutes later he burst into Daniel's office.

Sinclair was chatting with Daniel when John arrived. They both stood up. John was struck by the same feeling of intense familiarity as soon as he saw Sinclair. "This is my newly appointed assistant John Sanger," said Daniel. "You'll have to excuse his late arrival, we've all been working very hard to get things up and running."

"Not at all," said Sinclair. "So, did you major in parapsychology too, John?"

John had no idea. Daniel came to his rescue.

"John's currently doing his PHD on the history of poster art on the Tube. I hired him because he's actually a highly talented telepath and administrator."

"Poster art on the Tube," Sinclair said. "Is that right? I know of something that might interest you then. I imagine Daniel's told you that I run the UK's leading Electrical Installation and Maintenance group. We do a lot of work for the Underground so I have access to several disused stations on the Metropolitan line. They haven't changed since before the war, old posters on the wall and everything. You'll have to come and have a look sometime."

"I'd love to," said John.

Before he could give any more thought to Sinclair's disused station Daniel said, "I've just been telling Mr Sinclair about the plans for our little group of time travelers or 'Chrononauts' as we like to call them."

"Fascinating stuff," said Sinclair. "As soon as I came across Daniel's paper on Group Minds and Past Life Consciousnesses I knew I had to give him the funding for this project."

"I'm pleased to say Mr Sinclair's as passionate about our research as we are," said Daniel.

"I'm obsessed with time travel," said Sinclair. "I've read all the scientific and occult theories on the subject. This project is the closest thing I've seen to making it a reality. Looking out at the world of the past or the future through the eyes of someone who actually lives there. I'm not a telepath myself, but I envy you that opportunity."

"Do you mind me asking what's behind your interest in this field?" said John.

"No I don't mind at all. It's my legacy to future

generations. I'm afraid I won't be around to see the fruits of your research. A few months ago they found a tumour in my intestines. It's not operable. I have about a year left."

"I'm so sorry. I didn't realise or I . . . "

"That's all right, you weren't to know. The worst part is the feeling that you're trapped by some inescapable fate that you can do nothing to alter. That's why I'm interested in time travel. To conquer time is to master our own destinies. To transcend the boundaries of space and time so that no-one has to feel trapped by their fate again. Today I'm dying from a condition they'll be able to cure in the future. If we had time travel I'd be able to travel forward and save myself. When you think of the lives that your research might eventually save, you begin to see how important this work is."

"That's quite humbling," said John. "I can see you've given this a lot of thought."

"Mr Sinclair's extremely well informed in this area," said Daniel. "He was telling me before you came that time travel has a longer history than we realise."

"Many ancient civilisations believed there were hidden paths beneath time," Sinclair said. "That's why they built underground labyrinths and catacombs. They were a key to understanding these paths and a way of opening them. The druids practiced ritual disembowelment deep underground for just that purpose."

"Well I'm not sure the faculty will let us disembowel anyone," Daniel laughed. "Unless the Bursar's in a particularly bad mood." Sinclair laughed too and slapped Daniel on the back. It seemed like a friendly gesture but for a second a predatory look passed across Sinclair's face.

In that moment everything fell into place. John knew now why Daniel had panicked when they went to Sinclair's club. He'd worked out what Sinclair was doing. He hadn't threatened John outside the club, he was trying to warn him. Daniel wasn't the killer, Sinclair was.

Sinclair knew they were going to encounter a sub-dimension that ran beneath time. He planned to use it to travel to the future and save his life. He was going to sacrifice all of them to do so, down in his disused underground station. John had to find a way to stop this.

"I'm sorry," John said. "But I can't be a part of this any longer. I'd like to tender my resignation." He picked up his folder and left the room.

Daniel caught up with him in the corridor. "What on earth is going on?" he demanded.

"It's Sinclair, you've no idea how dangerous he is. He's going to kill us."

"You're not making any sense. Look John, you've obviously been working harder than I realised and I think the strain is beginning to show. Why don't you take a few days off and just rest up? We'll talk about this later."

John realised that nothing he said would convince Daniel. It all sounded too preposterous. He didn't have any proof, because nothing had happened yet. He suddenly felt powerless. He turned and ran from Daniel without saying another thing.

He got lost in the building again and ended up in the underground car park. He spotted the exit and made for it. He had to get out of the city and hide. Then he could try and expose Sinclair. It was the only way to stop it all happening again.

Complete silence settled on the car park. The lights at either end started to go out. John went cold. "No, not here," he said. "It shouldn't happen here. I haven't had enough time."

Rail tracks appeared in front of him and he heard the familiar screech and grind of the carriages coming into view. He pulled a piece of paper out of the folder and tried to write himself a note of warning about Sinclair, but the dark nothingness was eating up everything around him.

The doors opened and he boarded the middle carriage. The folder disappeared and he was back in a blood stained shirt and trousers. He glanced at the timeline. Nothing at all had changed. The futility of his efforts began to dawn on him. As soon as he climbed back on the carriage his old unwitting self would be back in charge of his life.

If he had left the city he would only have turned around and come back to his old life. If he had written a note he wouldn't have understood it. He would probably have put it all down to a temporary lapse of sanity.

He stared at the timeline and considered each of the stops with dismay. He could visit every one without significantly changing a thing. He would still end up stuck on this train speeding towards the End of the Line. He was trapped by an inescapable fate that he could do nothing to alter.

The walls of the carriage moved in on him. A vein throbbed in his temple and sweat soaked into his blood stained shirt. He tore the front of his shirt open, scattering the buttons. He roared and kicked the scuffed seats then punched the windows. If he could just shatter the glass he could at least try and jump off, but the glass wouldn't break and his knuckles were too sore.

"Stop the train," he shouted. "Do you hear me? I said stop it you fucking bastards STOP! Stop . . . stop it . . . please . . . please stop it please . . ." Tears spilled out of his eyes and his chest started to heave with sobs. "Just tell me what I have to do . . . please . . . just tell me . . . "

His stomach began to itch with an uncomfortable ferocity. He looked down and saw a huge scar forming.

***

He woke on the platform in a pool of blood.

He peeled his cheek off the ground and stumbled along the platform. He stopped beside the old wooden door. The whispering voices called out to him.

"You couldn't do it could you?"

"You tried and tried but nothing changed."

"You're trapped here and you can't do anything about it."

"Open the door."

"Open the door it's the only way out."

He took hold of the handle and the fear overcame him again. Fear of failure, of being unable to set things right, of having to admit this to his peers. But he was too tired and too beaten to fight the voices. The door opened inward with a screech of rusted hinges.

The stench made him gag, spoiled meat and blood wafted up. His eyes took a while to adjust to the dark and he didn't make out the corpses at first.

There were six of them piled up against the far wall. Each one had its stomach torn open and its intestines pulled out. He peered through the gloom and saw that the intestines were all hanging from metal pegs hammered into the wall.

The thick pink tubes were stretched out into straight lines that occasionally curved back on themselves, formed loops or crossed one another diagonally. In places the glistening flesh was torn and leaked blood or pus. Something about the shape they made was familiar. Then it hit him. The intestines were forming a crude replica of the Tube map.

He looked down at the corpses and there in the middle of them he saw the body of John Sanger wearing a blood stained shirt and torn trousers.

But that didn't make any sense. How could he be looking at his own corpse?

"You aren't," said John's corpse. "You're not John Sanger and you never have been."

"Then who am I?" he asked.

"Isn't it obvious," said a corpse he recognised as Michael Sayles. "You're the one who's responsible for all this."

Wait, he was Sinclair? Yes of course he was. It was all coming back to him. He was Sinclair and the corpses . . .

" . . . are your handiwork," said John's corpse. "Your first attempt at time travel. But it didn't go so well. You knew you needed a group mind to find the sub-dimension and a group sacrifice to open it. What you didn't know is that the tunnel won't lead anywhere without the group mind to guide you. You didn't transcend time and space, you erased yourself from them. You're trapped and you killed the only people that could save you."

"Not that you'd listen to us anyway," said Daniel's corpse. "You never do. Even now you're trying to use the spell to go back into our lives and change them so you can alter the outcome and get to the future."

"It won't work," said John. "It never does. As soon as you get inside our lives you lose all perspective. You forget who you are and what you're doing. You make the same mistakes over and over again."

"You didn't conquer time, Sinclair," said Daniel. "You're not the master of your own destiny. You're trapped by the fates of your victims and all you can do is relive them time and time again."

Sinclair ignored their prattling and concentrated on the intestinal tube map. He didn't need their guidance to fix this. He'd already proven how superior he was to all of them. The map was a key to the sub-dimension. He remembered now. It was also part of the spell that kept the corpses reanimated. Sadly he needed them in this state and he hadn't found a way to silence them yet.

He just needed to change the right moment in the right victim's life to change the working and get to the future. Sinclair studied the intestines and picked another victim. He focused his will on entering the victim's life and slipped into a trance.

He let go of his consciousness. He let go of his identity and found himself falling
falling
falling without end . . .

He woke on the platform in a pool of blood.

DEAD SCALP

CHAPTER 1

"**O**KAY," SAID CLEM. "Y'all have heard the charges agin Charlie McKinnell, made by the Judge himself—Big Bill."

Big Bill, who was tall, fat and had a streak of meanness even longer than his massive beard, grunted impatiently. He was warning Clem to move things along.

"Charlie stands accused o' peddling swamp root tonic behind Big Bill's back. Anyone gonna speak for the defense?" Clem scanned the bar of Big Bill's saloon. Nearly the whole of Dead Scalp was gathered for Charlie's trial. Not a one of 'em spoke up. They pulled at their beards and stared at the floor, trying not to catch Clem's eye.

All except for Tom Hill, who stepped away from the bar. Nat Mullens put a hand on his shoulder but Tom shrugged it off. "I will," said Tom. Bart Sommers, the only man in the room taller, fatter and worse smelling than Big Bill, grabbed Tom by his ginger beard and yanked him forward.

Bart put a cut throat razor to the bottom of James' beard. "D'you swear by yer whiskers, not to lie nor feed us any bull?" Tom swallowed. "Sure do," he said with a dry throat. Bart pushed Tom towards Big Bill and he fell at his feet. Bill leaned forward in his large leather chair.

"The witness has been sworn in," said Clem. "So let's hear his testimony."

Tom got to his feet and cleared his throat. "Well, if it please the court," he said. He glanced nervously at Bill. His expression froze into terror and pain at the deafening discharge of the Colt in Big Bill's hand. A single trickle of blood ran from the hole in Tom's forehead as the back of his head exploded.

"Aww Christ!" said Billy Williams jumping with pain as the bullet that passed through Tom, clipped his shoulder. Tom's brains were dripping from Billy's beard.

"Well," said Clem. "I guess the case for the defense rests."

"Yeah," called a voice from the back. "Rests all over Billy Williams." Everyone laughed at this, apart from Billy, who scowled and picked the bloody, pink globs from his whiskers.

"Quiet!" roared Big Bill and the laughter died in everyone's throat. "This ain't no laughing matter." The whole bar looked solemn as Bart dragged Tom's corpse out back to be burned.

Clem watched Big Bill eye Charlie, a thin, weasley guy with a straggly beard and a lazy eye, who was trussed up to a chair in front of Bill. "Ya got anythin' to say 'fore I pass sentence?" said Bill.

"Damn right I do," said Charlie. "How come I'm the only one up here, on trial. What about that bastard injun huh?"

"Rivers Flow?" said Bill. "Don't worry, I fixed him good."

Big Bill had fixed him all right. Clem had seen to it. He'd ordered the men at the ranch to butcher the injun's two boys, the ones Rivers Flow had with the young Mexican widow he took in.

Nothing came in or out of Dead Scalp without passing through the old injun's hands. This was the first time in four decades he'd been caught doing something behind Big Bill's back.

Big Bill needed Rivers Flow alive, but he had to learn he couldn't cross Big Bill. Charlie didn't have a hope.

"What about Nat then?" Charlie whined. "How come you ain't tried him?"

"Cos Nat admitted everything and you didn't, Charlie," said Bill. "You lied to me. Nat knew the game was up and he came clean. Turned evidence agin you. Told us how the whole set up was your idea."

Charlie struggled and strained to turn his head in Nat's direction. "Why you two faced, mother fucking son of a rattle snake! Why'd you go and double cross me? You know it wasn't all my idea at all. Lemme outta these ropes and I'll show you whose idea it was. I'll beat the truth outta the rat bastard."

"Already been done," said Big Bill. Nat, a short feller whose hair and beard were jet black, sunk low in his chair and winced from the bruises he was hiding. He was about the only feller in Dead Scalp who looked more weasley than Charlie.

"So that's it then," said Charlie. "You're gonna string me up and hang me out to dry, is that it?"

"Nope," said Bill. "We ain't gonna string you up."

"You're . . . you're gonna let me go?"

"I'm gonna make an example of you. The court hereby sentences you to death by ingrowing."

Charlie's eyes bugged and his jaw dropped. Most people in the room caught their breath. Clem had a cold sinking feeling in his gut and the temperature in the bar seemed to plummet. "What?" said Charlie. "You're joking ain't ya?"

"Do I look as though I'm joking?"

"Look Bill, I fucked up, I admit that. So just hang me, okay. Shoot me, slit my throat if ya must but not that, please . . . not that."

"Sorry, Charlie," said Bill standing and walking to the bar. "But I gotta make an example of ya." Bill reached behind the bar and pulled out a pot of glue and Charlie's wanted poster. Clem could see the looks of terror on just about every face in the saloon. As Bill tacked the poster up, next to the other five behind the bar, Clem took his chance. He walked up to Bill and leaned in.

"Are you sure this is for the best, Bill?" said Clem, in hushed tones. "I mean, you know what happened last time. Is it worth the risk?"

Bill scowled at him. "The swamp root tonic is our biggest money making operation, and it's *legit*. I don't care what happened last time. I'm risking a lot more if I don't set a precedent here. Now go hold Charlie's head!"

Clem knew better than to question Bill twice. He walked round back of Charlie and grabbed his head as Bill approached with a razor. Charlie was shaking and fighting his bonds, trying to turn his head away from the razor. "Please Bill, please . . . it's me . . . Charlie. How long did we ride together, Bill? Please, just hang me. Hell, I'll even climb up on the scaffold and jump my goddamn self."

Bill took hold of one side of Charlie's mustache and sliced it clean off with the razor, making sure to leave no stubble. Charlie let out a shrill scream as the hair came off. Clem hadn't heard anything so high pitched since that little girl whose mother they shot, back in '68. Charlie was jerking his head about so much in Clem's grip, that Bill nearly cut through his top lip taking off the other part of the mustache.

"Fuck's sake, Clem," said Bill. Clem just gritted his teeth as Bill returned to the bar, took a big dollop of glue and stuck both sides of the mustache to Charlie's photograph on the wanted poster.

Charlie continued to scream as Bart dragged him off, still tied to the chair. The veins in Charlie's neck were throbbing and his eyes were darting wildly about the room. "For God's sake," he shrieked. "Somebody shoot me, please just fucking shoot me. Why won't anybody shoot me?"

"Wouldn't make any difference now," said Bart and disappeared into the back room with him.

The men in the bar got to their feet and started to shuffle out. Nobody caught anyone else's eye. They were all intent on getting home and locking themselves in.

Clem watched Bill as everyone filed out. He stood with his back to them all, staring up at the six posters behind the bar. Each one had a real mustache stuck to it.

CHAPTER 2

J AMES BRIGGS WIPED the blood from his knife
and sheathed it.

The hare at his feet was beginning to shimmer. It
was sliced perfectly in half, with all its innards
carefully arranged around it. Even the skull was
cleaved in two, so you could see the tiny brain inside.

James thought the shimmer was a heat haze at
first, but neither the sunbaked ground, nor the hare's
innards, were hot enough to give off such a haze. The
little pebbles, arranged in arcane symbols around the
hare's carcass, began to rattle and shake.

The shimmer got much bigger and moved up into
the air above the hare. It hurt James's eyes to look as
it rose, like a column, over the hare. As it grew, the
shimmering reminded James of long strands of
transparent hair, vibrating so fast he couldn't focus on
them properly. He had to keep looking away because
his mind couldn't accept what he was seeing.

When the long shimmering strands had risen to
about ten feet in the air, they started to part, like a pair
of curtains. As they parted they made a shape like a
button hole. The more James looked at it, the more it
reminded him of a pair of cunny lips. James chuckled

to himself. *Ain't never been a cunny I wanted to get into this bad*, he thought.

As the center of the shimmering parted further, James could see a place beyond. A place that wasn't anything like the plateau where he was currently standing. James found it easier to look at the place than the shimmering. Even still, it was disconcerting.

The shimmering pulled back even more and James could see two figures on horseback waiting in the place beyond. *Must be the welcoming committee*, he thought.

One of the guys was real big, with a long black beard and a huge belly, the black mare he rode was doing all it could to bear his weight. The other feller, on a palomino stallion, was shorter and had a thin wiry body, with the longest sandy colored beard John had ever seen. He decided right away that the shorter guy was the more dangerous of the two.

"Howdy," said the shorter guy. "You go by the name of James Briggs?"

"Who wants to know?"

"My name's Clem Sorrel, this ornery looking feller here is Bart Sommers. Rivers Flow tells me you're looking for safe passage?"

"Got most of Arizona on my tail," said James. "Can't make it to the Mexican border from here, so I need a place to lay low."

"Well we might be able to help you there. Course, there's a few things we're gonna need from you first."

"Yeah I heard about that." James reached into the saddle bag at his feet and pulled out a folded sheet of paper. He unfolded it and held it up for Clem and Bart to see. "This here's my 'Wanted' poster, with the five hundred dollar reward and everything. Got my photo on it, right here. Looking real purty ain't I?"

"Tie it round a rock and toss it through the portal here," Clem told him. James complied. Bart caught the package and took the poster off the rock. "I guess it looks like him," he said. "You got the money?"

James held up the saddle bag. "Ten thousand in silver dollars, right here."

"Toss it on through then."

"Reckon I'll just hold onto it till you let me in. Not that I don't trust you fellers or nothing, but I ain't no fool neither."

"Okay," said Clem. "Open up the bag and show us the cash." James unbuckled the saddle bag and showed them the contents. "You reckon that's ten grand?" said Bart.

"And a little to spare."

James smiled. "Well I reckoned I might need a little spending money."

"Where's Rivers Flow?" said Bart. "I don't see the ol' cuss."

"He went behind that boulder over yonder."

"Why'd he do that?"

"I don't know, you'd have to ask *him*."

Bart ran a hand through his beard. "I don't like it. The injun usually handles the whole exchange. Why ain't he here to do that now?"

"The portal's open ain't it?" said Clem. "Only Rivers Flow can do that."

"So why did he light out?"

"Considering what we just done to his sons, can you blame him? Would you want to face us after that?"

"He brought that on himself. If he loved those boys so much why'd he give 'em such stupid names?"

"Sun Shines and Grass Grows? Guess he had a sense o' humor."

"Well, I don't like it. 'Less that injun shows, I ain't lettin' this guy in."

"Why not? He showed us his poster, we know the law's after him. He's got the money. What's the difference?"

"What makes you all fired up to let him in? You know this guy?"

"No, but I'm a little light at the moment. Maybe I could do with the transporter's fee I get for bringing him in."

"You should spend less time at those card tables."

"Well I'll be sure and take that advice under consideration. Soon as I get my fee."

"If you two lovebirds have finished with your little tiff," said James, "could you see your way clear to finishing up our little transaction?"

"You watch your mouth, mister," said Bart and reached for his pistol. Clem put a warning hand on Bart's chest. "Don't be a fool!" He turned back to James. "Portal closes up in a few moments, so you'd be advised to make your way through as best you can. I ought to warn you though. Once you step foot in here, you can't leave, not ever."

"Ain't got nothing holding me here," said James. "I'd just as soon never see Arizona again."

He slung the saddle bag over his shoulder and reached out to the edge of the portal. As soon as his hand came into contact with the shimmering, a force shot up his arm and tore through his body. Every part of him vibrated, his muscles spasmed and went into convulsions. He yanked his hand away before he bit his tongue off.

Bart laughed. "Oh yeah, should've mentioned, don't touch the edges none or you'll regret it."

James nodded. "Thanks for the advice." The edges of the portal were beginning to come together and the space James had to get through was getting smaller by the second.

"Best hurry up now," said Clem. "You don't have much time left."

James took a few steps back, then took a running jump at the portal. He leapt, head first at the space between the shimmering columns. It was like jumping between the ripples in the surface of a lake. He cleared the closing portal but his right foot caught the shimmering edge. The intense vibrations tore up his right side and his body jerked violently. He landed badly, still twitching. His left shoulder ached and his chest was bruised from landing on the saddle bag.

Bart laughed as James got to his feet and picked up his saddle bag. The first thing that struck James about his new surroundings was how still they were. There was no movement of any sort, except for the two men and their horses.

In the plateau James had just left, there had been an intermittent breeze blowing from across the plains. Flies buzzed and birds circled beneath the slow moving clouds over head. Here the air felt stagnant. James couldn't breathe enough to fill his lungs. There was no depth of sound. It was like listening under water. Everything seemed frozen and unending. It was as though he were in a perpetual dream state.

James was just getting used to the new sensations when he heard the click-click of a hammer being pulled back. Bart was holding a pistol on him. It was an old model Colt from around 1860. Everything about the two men was antiquated. Their weapons, their clothes, the way they acted.

"Reckon I'll have that saddle bag," Bart said. He had the drop on James, there was little chance of him missing at this range. James didn't move.

"You can have the ten grand in silver dollars as we agreed."

"Nope, I think I'll take it all. Then leave ya to walk back to town." Bart pointed behind him. "It's two miles south."

"You get a fee for bringing me in, your man Clem just said. You don't need any more from me."

"We got overheads to cover. Your fee just went up. Now hand it over."

James held out the saddle bag with his left arm and slowly approached Bart. When he was four steps away he dropped onto one knee and, using the saddle bag to shield himself, reached for his knife. It was out its sheath and hurtling towards Bart before the big galoot had a chance to react.

Bart yelled as the knife went right through his wrist. He let off a shot involuntarily. Blood poured down his hand. Bart's mare panicked at the noise and James took the opportunity to charge Bart.

James pulled Bart's right foot out of the stirrup and pushed him out of the saddle. Bart swore and hit the dirt. Taking a chance, James rolled under the rearing mare and sprang on Bart, who was lying on his back. He brought his knee down on Bart's chest and was glad to hear a rib crack.

Bart, who stank real bad up close, winced with the pain. He tried a right hook on James who blocked it and pulled the knife out of Bart's wrist. He put the tip of the knife to the corner of Bart's right eye.

James heard another click and felt the cold steel of a rifle barrel at the base of his neck. "Now just a minute there, pardner," he heard Clem say. "We don't look too kindly on killing around these parts. It brings . . . well let's just call it—unwanted consequences. So why don't you just put that knife away."

"Why don't you put that rifle away?"

"Well now, I'm the one with the drop on you, so I don't reckon you should be telling me what to do."

"No? You're the one told me killing has unwanted consequences. So I don't think you're aiming to shoot. Whereas me, on the other hand, I just had someone try to rob me. So I'm willing to take those consequences if it means keeping my cash. So why don't you lower that rifle and I'll spare this sumbitch's life?"

James felt the rifle barrel leave his neck. He climbed carefully off Bart with his knife held out in front, in case Bart tried something. James grabbed his saddle bag and Bart's pistol. He took the reins of Bart's mare, calmed it and climbed into the saddle. "I ain't the one who's gonna walk back to town," he said to Clem. "You got a problem with that?"

Clem just smiled. "See you back at town, Bart," he called over his shoulder as he rode off.

"Fuck you," said Bart as he dusted himself down.

***

"So how long've you been here?" James said, riding up alongside Clem and scratching his chin. His stubble was growing at a rapid pace.

"Around forty years now," said Clem.

198

"Forty years, are you sure? You don't look a day over thirty, even with the beard."

"Physically I'm twenty nine, but I've lived for sixty nine years."

"I don't follow you?"

"That's the effect Dead Scalp has on you. You don't age, you don't fall sick, so long as you ain't fool enough to get yourself killed, you could live forever."

"Forever?

"If you've a mind to."

"Oh, I've a mind to all right."

"Well you just made an enemy of one o' the most dangerous sumbitches in these parts. I'd be careful if I was you."

"He don't scare me none. I can handle myself."

"You can handle yourself all right, I'll give you that."

"So what's with the long beards then? Does everyone round these parts have one?"

"Yep, hair's about the only thing that grows here. Don't have no trees, nor plants, all we got's our locks and our beards."

"Well I'm aiming to visit the barber soon as we get to town."

"Don't have no barbers in Dead Scalp. Nobody shaves nor cuts their hair. You'd be advised not to yourself."

"Let me guess, it has certain consequences."

"Damn right it does."

They came to the head of a bluff. Below them, on a level plain, sat the ramshackle town of Dead Scalp. A rough collection of wooden buildings and unpaved streets.

"So is everyone in Dead Scalp an outlaw?" said James, as Clem led him down a narrow trail to the town below.

"Sure do ask a lotta questions don'cha," said Clem, with a wry smile.

"I'm about to hand over ten thousand dollars for the privilege of livin' here. Reckon I'm entitled to a few answers."

"Nope, they ain't all outlaws, only half the population's on the run from the law. They got in like you did. As to the rest, we got a lot of whores. Some of those came willingly, others were captured and forced to work in the brothels, bit like the slaves."

"Niggers you mean?"

"Not just the colored folk. We need men who can build and make things, carpenters and smiths. Mostly we kidnap 'em and force 'em to work for us. If they live long enough to work off the ten grand entry fee, we set 'em free."

"You let 'em go home?"

"No, they can't go home. Like I warned you, 'fore you got here, there's no way back. Once you're here, you're here forever."

"So how does a man make a fortune in this town?" said James as they reached the end of the trail and approached the first buildings.

"There's a few rackets," said Clem. "We always need stuff from the outside. Can't grow shit here, 'cept hair, so we gotta find ways to get food and liquor in without alerting the law."

"I can do that."

Clem steered his horse to one side as they came up to the saloon. James followed him. "Course you gotta give over half of everything you make to Big Bill," said Clem nodding to two men sitting out front of the saloon. The men nodded to others across the street. James was suddenly aware of at least five men reaching for their weapons.

"Big Bill," said James. "He the man that runs this place?"

"Let's just say he's not the man you wanna cross," said Clem with a broad smile. James could see five rifles trained on him. He scanned the street looking for routes of escape and froze when he felt a pistol barrel pressed against the base of his spine. Some guy had snuck up behind James without him even seeing or hearing.

"Speaking of which," said Clem. "I believe you were gonna hand over thirteen grand."

"Agreed price was ten."

"Well I just put it up. You put Bart out of action for at least a month. Big Bill ain't gonna be pleased. Muscle like Bart is hard to come by."

"That don't leave me hardly anything left."

"Been an expensive day for you then."

James handed over the saddle bag and filled his pockets with the coins he had left over. He'd been right about Clem. He was the more dangerous. "Been a pleasure doing business with you," said Clem. "Now you'll have to excuse me, I got some business to attend to, in a back room."

CHAPTER 3

Cᴌᴇᴍ ɴᴇᴇᴅᴇᴅ ᴛᴏ get a little drunk before attending to the business in the back room. Not so drunk he lost his edge, just enough to hold his nerve.

Doc Hendry let Clem into the back room. Charlie's corpse was laid out naked, on a long wooden table. Clem could see the ingrowing had started. There wasn't a hair left on Charlie's body. All of it had gone, including his beard.

The skin around his chin and scalp was the most raw. It was stretched out of shape by the hair that had forced its way back into his body. Charlie's eyeballs were bugging out of their sockets. Blood was streaming from his ears, his nose, his mouth and asshole. It had pooled around the body and was dripping off the table.

The two slaves in the room were staring at Charlie's body with terror. They were both young and new to Dead Scalp. They knew nothing of the ingrowing. That's why they'd been chosen to help with what came next.

"You boys all right?" said Clem. "I don't need to have you beaten or nothing do I?"

"No, sir," said the tallest, a skinny boy with a wispy blond beard. "We're fine. It's just, he was screamin' something awful afore we untied him. Then the screamin' kinda choked off and blood started pourin' outta him."

"That's cos the hair was all inside him," said the Doc. "First it would've crushed his lungs, then ruptured all his internal organs. It's a painful process. This case was kinda fascinating though. Never seen so much hair disappear so quick."

Doc's beady little eyes glittered behind his spectacles. He was a short, thin guy, with a bulbous red nose, who could come off kinda creepy. Especially when he appeared to relish these kinda details. Clem remembered he'd once been a man of science though, back before the drink and the back street abortions had put an end to his career. This was just the sort of thing that *would* fascinate them science guys, Clem figured.

"You get the swamp bark and the matches like I told ya?" Clem said to the shorter slave.

"Yes, sir," he said, fumbling with a big wooden bowl and dropping the matches. Clem cuffed him hard round the back of the head.

"You drop them matches one more time boy and I'll shoot you, understand? Little slips like that will get us all killed.

The skin over Charlie's belly started to swell and writhe, as though Charlie were suddenly pregnant with some hellish beast. Clem felt a sick, nervous feeling in the pit of his gut and wished he was a lot more drunk. "This here's the bit I hate," he said.

Blood began to pour in torrents out of Charlie's ass. Then his stomach sagged and sank back to its normal size as the first hairs poked their way out of his butt.

The hairs acted as if they were alive. They probed the top of the table and the inside of Charlie's thighs. They reared up as if scenting the air and moved towards the edge of the table. Huge wads of hair pushed their way out of Charlie's ass, stretching and splitting the puckered brown skin of his hole.

The hairs grabbed hold of the edge of the table and wrapped themselves around its legs. They moved further abroad, stretching themselves out of Charlie's torn anus and moving across the room. They grasped hold of loose floorboards, doorjambs and window bars. They snaked round the stove in the corner and cottoned on to anything in the room that would give them a purchase.

The two slaves had backed into one of the only two corners where the hair hadn't fastened itself. Clem and Doc stood in the other. "What . . . what in tarnation is happening," said the taller slave. "This is unbearable!"

"Shaddap," said Clem. "It gets a hell of a lot worse."

Once the hairs had all attached themselves to something, they began to tug at Charlie's asshole. More blood poured out as Charlie's innards were torn from his rectum. Charlie's legs were splayed with the pressure the hair was exerting. They stuck out at right angles to his body. Clem could hear the tendons and muscles in his hips snap and grind as the legs began to move into an even more impossible position. Charlie's arms began to move next, reaching straight up, while his shoulders contracted into his body with an awful noise.

Then Charlie's skull collapsed. His face folded into itself, and what was left of his head slithered down the bloody maw that was now his neck. Most of the interior of Charlie's body had been torn out of what had once been his asshole. With one huge, almighty tug the hair turned the rest of his body inside out.

What now lay on the table, was a writhing mass of living hair, ruptured organs and dislocated human bones. The taller slave let out a whimper.

"Light that goddamn bark and get over here," said Clem.

"It won't catch," said the short slave, holding it over a lit match. "I'm tryin' but it won't catch."

"Hold the match along the edge," said Clem, "not in the middle." The slave did as he was told and the dried bark finally caught light.

"Now blow out the flame and waft the smoke over that thing's body."

"Why?"

"Don't ask stupid fucking questions boy, just do as you're told. The smoke from that bark is the only thing that can knock this thing out and keep it under control. But we've got to act quickly, while it's still sluggish."

Doc Hendry was filling a big glass syringe with enough strychnine to kill a herd of buffalo, as the slave blew out the flaming bark and edged closer to the thing on the table.

It wasn't as sluggish as Clem thought. The slave didn't see the strands of hair that wrapped themselves around his ankle until his leg was yanked and he toppled to the ground, dropping the bowl with the bark.

More strands of hair caught the bowl and turned it over, trapping the smoke inside. The slave clawed at his throat in desperation as further strands of hair wrapped themselves around it, crushing his larynx and choking him to death.

Clem made a lunge for the bark in the upturned bowl. He didn't see the strands of hair that had pulled the barred grill off the window, until they swung the grill at his head. Bright sparks rattled around Clem's skull as the pain of the impact blinded him.

He may have passed out for a second. He heard breaking glass and guessed the hair was smashing the window with the grill. When he opened his eyes, he saw Doc Hendry make one last attempt to stick the thing with his syringe as it pulled itself out of the broken window.

Doc didn't spot the hair at his feet until it was pulled from under him like a rug. He fell on the tall slave who was curled into a ball in the corner. The Slave gasped when he saw the empty syringe sticking out of his chest.

"Sorry kid," Doc said as the slave frothed at the mouth and went into death spasms.

Clem put his hand to the throbbing lump on his temple and winced. He lay still for a moment contemplating what was worse. What that thing was going to do to Dead Scalp now it was loose, or what Big Bill was going to do to Clem when he found out it had escaped.

CHAPTER 4

JAMES HAD BEEN nursing the same glass of whiskey for over an hour now. He had to, it cost a damn sight more in Dead Scalp than it did on the outside. But then, everything seemed to cost a damn sight more in Dead Scalp.

Not for the first time that night, he wished he'd taken more silver dollars in the heist. It had been such a risky move though. Everyone had said it couldn't be done, that the place had too many men and was too well guarded, but James was desperate, and up against it.

The lawmen had gotten hold of a witness who was willing to testify that James shot Robert Perkins in a card game. Even though Perkins had it coming, John Law had a reason to see James swing.

After that, James's only hope of survival had been Dead Scalp. The lawmen had closed off the border so he couldn't get out of the country and the net was closing in on him. He'd heard the rumors about a mystical hideout that the law couldn't touch, the only problem was his lack of the entry fee—ten grand in silver dollars.

So James had staged a desperate robbery. The one

theft no-one thought was possible. James had nothing to lose, so he thought what the fuck. It was this or the scaffold.

Looking back he couldn't believe how easy it was. He'd been real careful to stay out of sight when he staked out the old ranch house. Even still, it felt as if the old devil in charge of the place had known he was there.

More than that, it was as if he were purposefully tempting James to come on down and make his move. He left doors unlocked and the gates off the hook. He moved the dogs out of the back yard and he got the guards blind drunk on moonshine.

It looked as though he wanted James to rob the place.

When James had struck, the old devil didn't put up any fight. Not even to save the drunken guards. He just stood by and watched as James blew their addled brains out. When James had put his gun to the old devil's head, he'd shown him exactly where the money was.

James's only mistake was not stealing more saddle bags and more horses. He'd made off with as much as he thought he could carry to Dead Scalp. It had all gone without a hitch.

Well not quite without a hitch. There'd been that slight business at the end, but that didn't matter now. He was here in Dead Scalp and the law could never touch him again. He was going to get rich and live forever and that's all that mattered. So long as no one found out he had nothing to worry about.

James's thoughts were cut short by the sound of feet approaching his table. He glanced up and saw Clem bearing down on him along with a man who was nearly as tall and fat as Bart. His beard was bigger though and he looked about the most dangerous man in a room filled with nothing but dangerous men. He had to be the guy who ran things.

James looked down at his drink and tilted his Stetson so they couldn't see his eyes. He heard them stop at his table. Surely they couldn't have found out already. There was no way that was possible.

"This him?" said a deep, rasping voice.

"Yeah that's him," said Clem's voice.

"Help you fellers?" said James without looking up.

"Yeah," said the raspy voice, which obviously belonged to Big Bill. "I hear tell you took out one of my men."

"Already paid off that debt," said James.

"I'll tell you when you've paid me off," said Bill in a voice that made James look up with a start. "Until then you owe me, understand?"

James blinked. He glanced from Bill to Clem, who had a huge bruise on his forehead, trying to read their eyes for suspicion. He saw nothing but anger in Bill's eyes but, for a moment, he was sure Clem had seen the fear behind his own eyes. "Reckon I do at that," James said. Bill wasn't a man you argued with.

"Now," continued Bill. "Clem here says you can handle yourself and I got something that needs handling."

"There any money in it?"

"Let's just say you'll be more likely to live if it goes well."

"That ain't the worst offer I've had since I got here."

"Good, you start straight away. Clem'll fill you in on the details."

"So you want me to work for you cos I took out your main muscle. Is that right?"

"No, I want you to help me sort something out, cos you're the new man in town, and that makes you too dumb to realize how scared you oughta be."

Big Bill turned and strode away. Clem smiled at him. "C'mon," he said. "It's already dark and you're not gonna like this."

CHAPTER 5

NAT WAS SHIT faced. What's more he was up two grand from the poker tables. Life was good.

He'd almost forgotten how bad he felt about poor Charlie and Tom. He'd done what had to be done though. He'd taken a pretty bad beating at the hands of Bill and his men and he had to give someone up. Charlie was the obvious scapegoat. Poor kid always was too trusting.

It was Nat's idea to run a side operation and cut Bill out. Charlie had been real scared of Big Bill discovering their racket. So Nat promised Charlie that, if anything happened, he'd take the fall. Charlie had bought it too.

The side operation only seemed fair to Nat. After all it had been him and Charlie who'd discovered the miraculous properties of the swamp water.

Charlie knew an old quack who ran a medicine show on the outside. He and Nat had bottled some of the stagnant water from the swamp on the outskirts of Dead Scalp, a sodden and fetid stretch of land next to the graveyard.

The first load of bottles damn near killed anyone who drank 'em. Then someone poured it over their head and discovered it not only cured baldness, but dandruff and head lice too. After that Nat and Charlie couldn't bottle it quick enough to satisfy the demand.

When Big Bill found out about this, he not only took his cut, but moved in and took over the whole operation. Nat and Charlie were frozen out. So Nat cut a side deal with Rivers Flow to help him move some bottles without Big Bill knowing.

Rivers Flow controlled all the traffic in and out of Dead Scalp. He was pissed enough at Bill's high handed ways to go along with it. Then Bill found out what they were pulling, and all three of 'em were in a world of trouble.

Nat never thought Bill would kill Charlie when he sold him out. He felt plenty cut up about it. It was a rotten shame. Charlie had been the only person in the whole Dead Scalp that Nat gave a shit about. The kid always did have a way of getting right under Nat's skin.

Charlie had called Nat two faced. Well he was right. But then, what did he expect? Nat was an outlaw for Christ's sake. People talked about honor among thieves but it didn't mean shit when it came down to it.

Saying one thing to someone, and doing something else behind their back, was what had gotten Nat where he was today. Damn right he was two faced. Two faced and proud of it.

Nat stumbled back towards his lodgings. He was tottering as he entered the dark alley that led to the room where he flopped. He had to prop himself up against the wall and feel his way down the alley.

Nat decided he must be really shit faced. The walls and the ground felt all spongy. No, not spongy, more soft and fibrous like . . . like . . . oh shit!

Strands of hair wrapped themselves tight around Nat's ankles, making it impossible for him to flee. More strands wrapped themselves around his wrists.

"Charlie . . . Charlie, is that you?" said Nat. "Oh Christ Charlie, what have they done to you?" Charlie didn't answer, but Nat felt hundreds and hundreds of individual hairs wrap themselves around the hairs of his head and beard.

"Now listen, Charlie, I know I ratted you out and everything, but honest to God, if I'd known what Big Bill was gonna do to you I never would've said a word." Nat felt more hairs wrap themselves around his own.

"Well okay, I might have said *something*, but I wouldn't have let you take all the blame—"

Nat's words were cut short as the living hairs tugged fiercely at his beard and hair, stretching the skin of his face so taut he could neither blink nor open his mouth to scream with the pain.

Nate saw something glint in the moonlight. It was a shard of glass being held by a bunch of hairs. The hairs brought the shard of glass up to Nat's face and buried it in the top of his forehead, just below his hairline.

A sharp, hot agony shot through Nat's face as the hair forced the shard of sharpened glass down, slicing through the skin of his forehead. Then down his nose, through his top and bottom lip and finally over his chin and throat.

Blood streamed from the deep cut in the center of his face. Nat gasped with the shock of the wound and breathed in the blood through his nose and mouth, making him cough violently.

The other hairs were still tugging at his hair and

beard. Nat felt the skin of his face begin to peel away from the bones and cartilage of his skull.

As the pain reached a new, burning intensity, more hairs forced themselves through the gap in his face. They wriggled under his skin, scraping it away from the bone as they snaked around his skull. The part of Nat's mind that was still conscious refused to believe that this was happening to him. He couldn't accept that his old friend had become something so monstrous, something capable of doing this to a man. But then, the kid always did have a way of getting right under Nat's skin.

The hair wound its way under Nat's scalp, and moved further down beneath the skin of his neck and over the inside of his shoulders. It scoured the muscle like a thousand white hot filaments.

More hairs bunched up under the skin of Nat's face and tore it away from his skull, stretching it out as far as it would go. They burrowed into his eye sockets and wrapped themselves around his eyeballs.

With an insistent tug that sent a shaft of blinding hot pain through his brain, the hairs pulled the eyes from their sockets, but kept them behind the eyelids as they folded the torn skin of Nat's face in on itself.

Nat's mind had almost shut down with the torment. His eyeballs were still attached to their optic nerves. They were still sending images to his shrieking brain. It took them a little while to process what they were seeing. But then it dawned on him, as the severed skin and eyeball, from one side of his skull, came face to face with the other.

Charlie had called Nat two faced. He was right, and in the last few moments of his life, both of Nat's faces got to take a good long look at each other.

CHAPTER 6

"HOW IN HELL does this thing move so fast?" James yelled as he cantered up to the graveyard next to Clem. He'd been roped into chasing the creature that used to be Charlie McKinnel and he'd seen what it had done to Nat Gunderson.

"Damned if I know," said Clem. "Where's the damned thing at? It was headed this way, couldn't have gone anywhere else."

"Why in hell do you have a graveyard anyway? You told me nobody dies here."

"Less they're shot or stabbed or some such."

"And you bury 'em here?"

"No, mainly we burn the corpses so they don't turn out like the thing we're chasing. But we can't burn things like this. The flames just won't take 'em. So we have to bury 'em. For some reason, this land next to the swamp has some kinda power over 'em, keeps 'em dead and buried. We burn the corpses right next to the graveyard for the same reason."

James reigned in his horse at the rough stone entrance to the graveyard. The land next to the swamp was damp and oppressive. The whole place felt old and very, very dead. "So you've had this happen before then? I mean, you've shaved some poor fucker's beard off and they've turned into one of these things?"

"Only when Big Bill really wanted to punish someone. And we've never had one get away before. They're usually easy to handle, so long as we burn the swamp bark to knock 'em out."

"How many times have you done this?"

"You've seen the posters behind the bar."

"Ones with the mustaches stuck to 'em?"

"That's right."

Doc Hendry rode up behind them. "Has it got here yet?" he said.

"Can't see it," said Clem.

Doc Hendry dismounted, lit the kerosene lamp from his saddle and peered through the entrance. "You ain't seen it cos you weren't looking in the right place."

"Waddaya mean?"

"Look, right here," said the Doc raising his lamp. James and Clem dismounted and joined him at the entrance. Doc pointed to the center of the graveyard.

Between the graves they saw what looked like some kind of twisted plant. As they peered closer, they realized it was the strange hair creature. It had somehow bedded itself into the damp soil of the graveyard. It looked like a giant clump of twisted flesh covered all over in impossibly long strands of hair. Its hair was snaking between all the graves, as if it had a mind of its own.

"What in God's name is it doing?" said James. "Is this normal?"

"Nothing about these things is normal," said Clem. "But I ain't never seen one do this before. Let's light up a bunch of swamp bark and take a closer look."

James watched Clem and Doc light their pieces of bark, then blow out the flames, so they were smoking. He wasn't certain how the bark might knock one of these monsters out, but he followed suit. Each of them held the bark in front of them as they entered the graveyard. The ground was soft and mossy and filled with water that soaked into James's boots.

The first thing James noticed was that there were eleven graves. "Hey," he said. "There are only six posters behind the bar, but there are eleven graves here."

"Think we were the first people to live here?" said Clem.

"There were others before you?"

Clem didn't answer. But he did put his arm up to stop James from moving any further forward. Clem pointed at the ground. James looked down and saw the ends of lots of hair stroking the front of his boot. Clem removed his arm and James slowly moved his foot back.

"Got to be careful," Clem said. "This thing is more dangerous than you can believe."

"I already seen what it can do."

"You ain't seen shit yet, boy."

Doc raised his lantern up. The thing was sinking further and further into the ground, burying itself in the soft, spongy earth. The body beneath all the hair started to ripple, like waves were passing through it. Then it started to go into convulsions and something shot out of it and flew at least fifteen feet up in the air.

James jumped back with shock and dropped his smoking bark. It landed next to the ends of some hair and they withdrew from the bark, pulling themselves rapidly backwards. *So the bark does have an effect on these things after all*, James thought.

James heard a wet thud behind them as he was picking his bark off the ground. He spun round and saw something burrow its way into one of the graves. The hair thing had another convulsion and something else shot from under its hair.

James took a step back onto one of the graves and craned his neck, trying to see what had shot out of the thing. Something warm hit him right in the forehead with a wet slap. He jumped and pulled the hot, slimy thing off his face.

It looked like a ruptured human liver, with all kinds of living hairs growing out of it. The liver wriggled in his fingers and he threw it at the ground in disgust. The organ crawled onto the grave at James's feet and started to dig its way into the soil.

"The hell is that?" said Clem.

"It looks like a liver with hairs," said James. "It's digging its way into this grave."

The liver had almost disappeared by the time Clem and Doc joined James at the grave to have a look. "I'll be darned," said Doc. They all turned to look back at the thing as it convulsed once again and shot something else into the air.

Doc followed the trajectory of the object and watched as it hit another grave. "What is it, Doc?" called Clem.

"Looks like a busted lung with hairs," Doc shouted back. "It's burying itself in this here grave."

"What the hell is going on?" said James.

"Fucked if I know," said Clem.

All three of them backed towards the entrance and

watched as the hair thing shot eight more busted and hairy organs into the air. Each of the organs landed on one of the graves and dug itself in. "Any idea what's going on, Doc?" said Clem.

"Well, I ain't certain, but my guess is that it's sporing."

"Sporing! What in hell does that mean?"

"It's what fungi do when they want to reproduce. They shoot hundreds of spores up into the air, hoping they'll land on a cow pat, or a rotting tree or whatever they grow on. I read a paper on it once, many years ago."

"I ain't ever read anything like that in the paper."

"This was a scientific paper."

"That thing's trying to reproduce?" said James. "Ya mean it's trying to have sex with the other corpses or something?"

"Well, I dunno about that, I was just hypothesizing."

"Hypothe-what?"

"I was just throwing ideas out there. It kinda reminded me of the paper I read on fungus spores is all."

James felt the ground shudder. They all turned to look at the thing, which was sinking into the sodden ground, dragging all its hair after it. Finally it sank from sight and there was no trace of it left.

Clem and Doc started to walk back into the graveyard, being very careful about where they trod. James followed them. When they got to the spot where the thing had bedded in, they found a mound of freshly moved earth and nothing else.

"Well that just saved us a whole heap of trouble,"

said Clem. He looked straight at Doc and James with a mean set to his face. "Listen, as far as Big Bill's concerned we dealt with this business and that thing is now good and buried in this graveyard, understand?"

"That's fine by me," said Doc.

"I got no arguments," said James.

"Good," said Clem. "Now let's get the hell outta here. I got whores to fuck and whiskey to drink."

James followed Doc and Clem out of the graveyard. Then he jumped in his saddle and rode back into town.

CHAPTER 7

I T WAS GETTING close to dawn when Bart rode up to the graveyard with the corpse of the woman dragging behind him. He had to butcher and burn the bitch himself now he'd fallen out of favor with Bill.

In the past, Bill would have sent one of his lackeys to dismember and burn the body. Bart hardly ever came out here, to this desolate spot by the graveyard. He'd sent more than a few bodies though, and more than a few lackeys. It wasn't usually whores that Bart murdered. Mostly it was guys that got in his way or looked at him wrong.

Bill had always turned a blind eye to his murderous rage, cos Bart was useful to him. Besides, it made men more afraid of Bart, and that made them more afraid of Bill, knowing he had a mad dog on a leash.

That was before James, that sneaky little shit, had side swiped him. Bart had limped back into town with a bruised shoulder, busted ribs and a wounded hand that was starting to go bad. Doc Hendry had fixed him best he could, but Bill wouldn't even see him.

He was out in the cold for the time being. But that would change. James might think he had everyone fooled but Bart knew better. He might have wangled his way into Bill's good books, trying to replace Bart, but he'd get the goods on him soon. There was something about James that wasn't right, and when Bart found out what it was, he was gonna fix him good and proper. He'd make James wish he'd never set foot in Dead Scalp.

Bart had been drinking while Clem and James were out chasing whatever Charlie McKinnell had become. If Bart had been in charge, the thing would never have escaped. Clem was slipping and James couldn't be trusted. Bill would find out, soon enough.

After he'd got good and drunk, Bart had gone round to Molly's brothel. Bart liked to break in the new girls, let 'em know what they could expect from now on. Many of 'em had been snatched from regular life and had never even sucked a dick before, let alone worked in a brothel.

Some of 'em were married, others even had jobs, like being a librarian or a school teacher. Bart couldn't believe how bad things were getting on the outside if they were letting women have jobs. There were some real uppity bitches among 'em. They'd put on all kinds of airs, making threats about what was going to happen when their disappearance was discovered.

No-one was coming for 'em though, they'd find out pretty soon. They'd never be found in Dead Scalp. They were gonna be whores for the rest of their lives, and if they didn't get themselves killed, those lives were gonna last longer than most.

Molly let Bart break 'em in for free. By the time he'd finished with 'em, they had a pretty good idea of what they had to look forward to. He enjoyed the ones who were full of fire and defiance at the beginning. By the time he was finished with 'em, they broke down and let him do whatever he wanted.

Bart had a talent for taming the bitches. He knew exactly how to find the source of their strength and self worth. Then he wouldn't just take it away from 'em. He'd destroy it utterly. After that you had a whore you could do pretty much anything you wanted with.

Bart had learned how to do this from his mother of all people. She'd raised him by herself and she had a way of honing straight in on a man's weakness. She'd done as much with Bart.

She'd never chided him for all the trouble he'd caused. Instead she'd pitied him his sinful ways. It cut Bart to his very core that, the things that caused the other kids to fear him, brought only pity from his mother.

She knew this, and she used it remorselessly. Made him feel small and insignificant, some failure to be looked down on. He grew to hate that pity and fear it. Fear it in his mother and any other human being he came across.

That's how Bart had turned out the way he did. He made people fear him, hate him and respect him, but he wouldn't tolerate pity in anyone. That's why he was so good at breaking the bitches in. He was paying each and every one of them back for the pity that his mother had terrorized him with.

Molly wouldn't let him have a girl for free when he'd turned up at the brothel. She'd greeted him personally and given him a bottle on the house, the real stuff too, not the watered down shit she gave to most customers. Then she'd explained to him, as sweetly as she could, that according to Bill's orders, Bart wasn't to get no more free pussy from now on.

Bart was close to beating her unconscious, but Molly knew her way around him. She assured him that it was only temporary, that he'd be back in with Bill in no time, and then she'd make certain to do something real special for him. But she had to ask him to pay just this once, cos she couldn't afford to get on the wrong side of Bill.

Bart had stood and thrown his coins on the floor to make certain Molly had to get down at his feet to pick the money up. Then he'd staggered into the dark room where the new arrival was chained to the wall.

Straight away she started into him. Calling him a filthy pig who stank. Telling him that nothing in the world would make her submit to his lustful demands. He smacked her around a little. Nothing that would break bones or knock her unconscious, just enough to make her see sense.

That didn't do a thing to shut her up though. She started screaming and calling him names. Asking him if this was the sort of man he was? The sort who had to beat a woman senseless before she'd agree to sleep with him.

Bart could see a more brutal approach was needed, so he pulled out his knife and put it to her throat, hard enough to draw blood. Then he pulled his cock out. She looked down at his stiff cock, swollen with blood, and she laughed. A bitter mocking laugh that made him wilt.

"Call that a cock?" she said. "My two year old boy has a bigger cock than that. You think I'm going to be scared of something that tiny?"

Bart really lost his temper then. It was one insult too many. He'd been in enough bath houses to know he was fairly well hung.

He couldn't take any more. He'd been forced to pay for his cunny. He'd been frozen out by Big Bill. And he'd been blindsided by that little pissant James Briggs. There was only so much humiliation a man could take.

So he took the knife and sliced through the bodice of her dress. Then he tore the material apart and sliced the straps on her brassiere. "Go on, take a good look you pig," she'd said as her breasts swung free.

Instead of touching her breasts and letting her mock him some more, he stuck the knife in the side of her body. She wailed in pain and outrage. Then she spat in his face and called him a worm. A tiny little worm who needs a knife to feel big.

Bart was filled with a blinding fury. He couldn't find her weak spot. Couldn't pin down what gave her such strength and self worth.

He stuck the knife in her stomach. She wailed again, even louder and this got Bart good and hard. Before she could spit at him, Bart pushed his cock into the bleeding gash in her stomach.

Her stomach wall gripped his dick real tight. He liked the way her blood felt dripping off his balls. He even liked the way her innards parted as he pushed his cock into 'em. But he hated the way she'd stared at him the whole time he was doing it.

Her stare spoiled the whole thing. He was fucking her to death, but he didn't feel at all powerful. She was dying, but her sneer had made him feel small and pathetic. He took his knife and stabbed it in her jugular, then sliced down the vein.

The blood sprayed both of them. A fierce jet that left him dripping with gore. The look on her face as she died had made his cock shrink. It wasn't the contempt that shone in her eyes as she died, it was the pity that cut him to his core.

In her dying moments the woman had pitied Bart. Pitied him worse than his mother ever had. Bart's cock shriveled quicker than if he'd been standing in a snow drift. It plopped out of her stomach and retreated up into his wrinkled ball sack till it was smaller than Bart had ever seen it.

At this point Molly walked in. Bart was actually crying as she entered. Tears ran down his cheeks and blood dripped from his tiny little dick. He knew, in that moment, that she no longer feared him. That he would never have power over her again. Not after she'd seen him like this.

"Bart honey, you best take that body up by the graveyard and burn it," Molly said. Bart nodded meekly. Then Molly unlocked the shackles and Bart dragged the body outside as if Big Bill himself had ordered it.

Bart tied the woman's ankles with rope, then fastened her to the saddle of the nag he kept as back up. Then he'd ridden off, dragging her bloodied corpse behind him.

Her body was a little beaten up by the time he got to the graveyard. In the dawn light he could see that, in spite of the damage the ride had done to her face, she was still looking at him with awful pity.

Bart climbed down from his nag and untied the rope from the horn of his saddle. He dragged the corpse up the tiny hillock next to the graveyard; the only spot of dry ground close enough to the graveyard to burn a body.

Bill walked over to the woodpile that was supposed to be stocked for just this sort of occasion. There was a tiny collection of logs and an even smaller pile of kindling. A half empty kerosene bottle sat next to the wood. Hardly enough to set light to a corpse.

Bart cursed his bad luck. Things were getting scarce in Dead Scalp lately. Surely Bill must know about this. How could he let stocks get so low? How could he let little shits like James steal Bart's place in Bill's favor?

Bart began to build a fire as best he could. He glanced on over at the graveyard. It looked kinda different. As if it had changed color. Then it struck Bart. He knew what was wrong. There was a brown carpet growing across the whole graveyard and out of the gates.

It looked like very fine brown grass sprouting up out of the ground. Bart blinked and looked again. That couldn't be right. No grass grew in Dead Scalp. Yet more and more of it was appearing all the time. It advanced up to the little hillock where Bart stood. Then he realized that it wasn't grass. It was hair!

Within seconds, hair started to sprout from the ground beneath Bart's feet. He dropped the wood and forgot about burning the woman's body. Bart ran for his horse as the ground all around him grew hair.

Before he could get to the nag, the hair at his feet wrapped itself around his ankles. Bart was held fast. He tried pulling with his legs and tearing at the hair with his hands, but he was unable to raise either of his feet.

For the first time in forty years, Bart was suddenly very scared. He didn't recognize the feeling at first. It crept into his gut like a chill weight. His chest rose and fell with heavy, convulsive breaths. Then Bart noticed how much he was sweating and it suddenly hit him. He was more scared than he'd been as a boy, when his mother had fixed him with her eye and he knew she was going to skewer him with her ice cold pity.

Bart had forgotten about fear since he came to Dead Scalp. He was the baddest motherfucker, in a magic town, where you never got old or died. He'd had nothing to be afraid of, until this very moment, when there was a sudden and growing likelihood of his death.

The hair sprouting from the ground wove its way up his legs and fastened onto his waist, unbuckled his belt and tugged his trousers to the ground.

"Mother fucker!" Bart shouted and grabbed at his pants, but they disappeared beneath the morass of hair that was surrounding him. The hair began to bind itself to his legs and hundreds of individual hairs wrapped themselves around Bart's leg hairs.

The hair worked its way up his legs from ankles to thighs. Bart winced as each leg hair was yanked, sending tiny pin pricks of pain up both his limbs. Bart glanced over at the corpse of the woman. The look of pity that was seared into her features seemed to have intensified and he saw his mother gazing out at him from her face.

Hair sprung up from the ground all around her. It folded itself over her limbs with a gentleness that could almost be mistaken for love. It rolled under her still form like a canopy and lifted her body from the ground.

Bart watched as the woman's body was passed

along the carpet of hair on a single ripple that moved from strand to strand and carried her back towards the graveyard. Bart saw that the graveyard, and the ground that surrounded it, were now covered with a luxurious lawn of hair. The lawn was spreading quickly and Bart could see it wouldn't be long before it reached the town. *God help those bastards when it hits*, he thought.

That brought him back to his own predicament. The hair growing over his legs had reached his crotch, and begun to fasten onto his pubic hair. First the hairs around his scrotum, then around his anus, finally the bush of hairs above his cock.

Every attempt Bart made to stop the hair's progress brought him more torment. The hair pulled on the follicles they were already torturing, and refused to let go, no matter how desperately he clawed at them.

The strands that had a tight hold of his short and curlies separated themselves from the others. Then they began to retreat back into the ground. Bart was pulled into a squat. His crotch throbbed with the pressure the hair was exerting.

The agony was so great he hadn't even noticed the hair that had crept under his shirt and taken hold of the hairs up his back. Not until it began to pull him backwards, and away from the hairs that were tugging at his crotch, was he aware it was even there. By then it was too late.

Bart screamed and cussed in anger and pain, and tore at the hair coming out of the ground around him, like a foul mouthed toddler trying to pull up grass. He was as helpless as a squalling infant in the hands of a parent who means to teach it a hard lesson.

For a moment this scared Bart more than the damage the hair was doing to his body. Then a deeper, fiery pain burst from the skin around his crotch. It wasn't until Bart heard the rending, and smelled the blood gushing down the insides of his thighs, that he looked down and saw the skin above his bush had torn and was coming away from his body.

Bart suddenly felt very cold and his mind disconnected itself from what was happening to him. The disbelief cushioned him from the shock of what was being done to his body. The tear in his skin widened and travelled along the sides of his scrotum then around the back of it.

The full extent of what was occurring only hit Bart when he watched the base of his foreskin fold over on itself and peel away from his penis, like the sleeve of a sweater turned inside out. The pink erectile tissue and the bright red glans beneath looked so delicate and fragile that Bart sobbed with pity for his cock. Then despised himself for feeling the one emotion he hated most of all.

Bart's scrotum detached itself and his testicles plopped out. Two pink and white ovals dangling from red and brown, tubular ducts. The inside of his dick looked soft and moist in the dawn light. More hairs wrapped themselves around what was left of Bart's reproductive organs and yanked them so hard they ruptured and tore away from his body.

Bart howled with rage and anguish as blood flooded from his loins and pooled beneath him. He was livid about everything that had been taken from him. Since Charlie McKinnell's death, the hair had taken his income, his power, and now his manhood.

The hair had known exactly how to find the source of his strength and self worth. But it hadn't just taken it from him. The hair had destroyed it utterly.

Bart just hoped he bled out before anyone found him. If they did find him alive, they'd have a man you could do pretty much anything they wanted with. Except pity him. Dear God don't let them pity him.

CHAPTER 8

$\int$AMES WOKE SLOWLY. He'd drunk himself to sleep the night before, and he was wary of the hangover that might be waiting, when he opened his eyes.

He'd needed the alcohol to wash away everything he'd seen last night. Like the mess that was left of Nat Gunderson. Or the strange hair creature trying to pollinate the graveyard with its ruptured organs, before it buried itself.

The way Clem had told the story, Big Bill had been pleased with all of them. So pleased, he gave James a night's lodgings in the saloon, and a free whore, who James was too drunk to use in the end. He could have made use of her now, if he didn't have such a splitting head.

James pulled back the cover and climbed off the horse hair mattress. *Horse hair*, he thought, and shuddered. He walked to the dresser at the foot of the bed, put his head over the earthenware bowl there, and poured a whole pitcher of water over his head.

This helped clear his head, but it didn't do anything to stop the pounding. He stared in the cracked mirror and stroked his chin. After one day here, he had a full grown beard and his hair was longer too.

That's when he heard the first scream. It was high pitched and hysterical. Probably a woman's scream, but James had heard men make similar noises in his time. It had come from outside on the street.

James pulled on his pants and walked through the saloon to see what the commotion was all about. What he saw on the street made his stomach lurch and sweat break out on the back of his neck.

All along the street hair was growing out of the ground, like a fine brown carpet or an auburn lawn. It was creeping up the sides of buildings like vines and breaking through the walls. Many of the people on the street were stuck fast to the ground. The hair had grown over their feet and around their ankles and was holding them tight.

James saw two women fighting over a ladder that could have led them both to safety, if they'd helped each other, as long strands of hair reached up from the ground and engulfed them both. He saw a man clubbing a horse till he drew blood, as the trapped horse whinnied and bucked in desperation at the hair that was wrapping itself around its legs.

Doc Hendry was trying to make his way to the saloon. He was holding the tiny lump of swamp bark that he had from last night. Great clumps of hair were rising up all around him like brown, fibrous waves. Doc would wave the smoking bark at one clump, to ward it off, and another clump would loom ominously over him. Doc would then have to fend that clump off while the first closed in on him.

He was within ten feet of the saloon when an unseen clump grabbed him round the middle like a tentacle and lifted him off his feet. Doc yelled and dropped the bark. The tentacle dragged him under an ocean of undulating hair.

"Let go of my fucking leg!" James heard a familiar voice growl. He turned to see Big Bill and Clem advancing through the hair towards the saloon. They were both carrying Civil War sabers. They used them to hack at the surrounding hair like machetes slicing through foliage. As each new tendril of hair reared up over them they attacked it with the blade.

A woman had hold of Big Bill's legs. Great lengths of hair had wrapped themselves around her legs and waist. She was lying prostrate and her fingers dug into Bill's leg. Her face was etched with terror and pleas for help.

"I said let go!" Bill snarled. He brought his saber down on her forearms, severing them just below the elbow. The woman screamed as the hair dragged her into its seething undergrowth. Within seconds, all that could be seen of her were the stumps of her arms, spraying the hair red with blood.

Bill reached the steps of the saloon. As he was mounting them a tendril of hair seized his right wrist preventing him from wielding the saber. Another tendril grasped his left shoulder and began to tug him back.

James rushed from the doorway and snatched the saber from Bill's hand. He chopped at the hair that held Bill prone. It was tougher than it looked and the saber's blade was chipped from severing the woman's arms. Finally James hacked his way through the hair. "About fucking time," Bill said as the hair fell from his wrist and shoulder.

James ran up the steps after Clem and Bill. Before

he could get back into the saloon he heard a thump behind him. He turned to see Doc Hendry standing on the top step. The skin of Doc's hands and face seemed stretched and misshapen, as though something was writhing beneath it.

Blood trickled from Doc's nostril and the corner of his mouth. His eyes were filled with an inexpressible pain and his movements were strange and jerky, as if he weren't in control of his body. Between Doc's legs, James caught sight of a thick cable of hair that appeared to be fixed to his back. James's mouth went dry as he realized that the hair had torn a hole in Doc's back and forced its way beneath his skin while he was still alive. It was using Doc as a living meat puppet.

Before James could say anything, Clem moved towards Doc to help him. Doc's head jerked backwards and there was an audible click as his jaw dislocated and his mouth opened impossibly wide.

Clem froze as he realized something was wrong. Hair streamed out of Doc's mouth, dripping with Doc's blood and saliva. It latched onto Clem's own hair and entwined itself inextricably about it. The cable of hair at the back of Doc began to retreat, taking Doc and Clem with it.

Clem cried out and stumbled forward, trying to dig his heels in and pull himself free. James caught hold of Clem's waist while Big Bill grabbed his shoulders. "Get it off, get it off," Clem screamed and hacked at the hair with his saber.

"You can't cut your hair, that'll kill you," said Bill, reaching into his boot for a knife. Bill took hold of Clem's chin and put the blade against the top of his forehead. James watched in horror as Bill cut into the skin and sliced along Clem's hairline. Clem yelled with pain as a thick veil of blood spilled over his face. Bill continued to cut along the hairline, moving the knife around the back of Clem's head, then up the other side of his face and over the top of his ear.

The scalp started to peel away from the top of Clem's skull. Bill didn't need to cut through the last of it. It was torn from Clem's head as the hair from Doc's mouth shot back into his head. The hair at his back yanked Doc's body from the top step and engulfed it once again. James, Clem and Bill fell backwards through the door of the saloon. "Get him up to my office," Bill ordered as he got to his feet and stomped up the stairs.

Clem was twitching with shock as James lifted and dragged him towards the stairs. Clem's face was covered with a layer of blood so thick, James could only see the whites of his eyes and his bared teeth. The blood was starting to clot around the frayed edges of skin that clung to Clem's temples. James could see the white of Clem's skull beneath the gore that speckled it.

James dragged Clem up the stairs and through the door of Bill's office. Bill locked and bolted the door behind them and closed all the shutters on the windows. James laid Clem down on a couch; he appeared to be unconscious.

"I thought you said you sorted this thing out," Bill said.

"We did," said James.

"So why's my town covered in hair? Didn't you bury that thing properly?"

"Well, it kinda buried itself."

"What do you mean?"

"It was stuck in the ground of the graveyard when we found it. Then it started shooting its innards up into the air. The innards was covered in hair and they landed on the other graves and buried themselves. Doc Hendry said it was sporing, like a mushroom. Then it just sunk into the ground and disappeared."

Bill shook his head in disgust and disbelief. "I oughta kill both of you fuckers right here on the spot."

"Can't we just burn some of the swamp bark and drive all the hair back?"

Bill knelt in front of his safe and unlocked it. He removed a small burlap sack and emptied its contents on his desk. Twelve small pieces of bark sat on the desktop. "That's all the bark we have left. We've scraped every last piece of it off of the dead trees in the swamp, and that's all we have left."

"How come?"

"Cos nothing grows in this godforsaken place, that's how come. Nothing 'cept hair. Think we're gonna drive that murderous tide of hair back with just this?"

"No."

"Exactly."

Clem came round with a groan.

"You fucked up, Clem," Bill shouted at him. "You fucked up and look how things turned out. This isn't right though, it isn't right. It shouldn't be happening. I had assurances. You remember? Assurances! This place is mine now. Mine! As long as the sun shines, the grass grows and the rivers flow. That's what I was promised!"

Bill paced the floor of his office, tugging at his beard in thought. James knew enough to keep his mouth shut while Bill ruminated. "This is Tsiishch'ili's doing I'll swear it is. It's got his name written all over it. If I could put my hands round his stinking throat all over again . . . Wait . . . that's it . . . I'll summon up the conniving redskin, that's what I'll do. I've still got all the stuff to do it."

He turned to James. "You look after Clem. I've just got to go get some stuff from the other room. Don't let anyone in till I get back." With that, Bill left by a connecting door to one of the other rooms.

Clem groaned again, and his eyelids fluttered. James shook him to keep him conscious. "Clem, stay with me, Clem. What was Big Bill talking about? Is this place really his? What did he mean he had assurances?"

Clem licked his lips with a dry tongue. His breathing was little more than a rasp. "There's some whiskey in the bottom drawer of Bill's desk," he said. "Real good stuff, single malt, bring it to me."

"Won't Bill be mad?"

"Think I give a fuck what Bill thinks? Fetch me that whiskey and I'll explain everything."

James got the whiskey from the bottom drawer and Clem took a good long pull on the bottle. He sighed and wiped some of the blood from his eyes. "What Bill means is that he had assurances from the injuns who were here before us."

"This place used to belong to the redskins?"

"Whole damn country used to belong to the redskins."

CHAPTER 9

CLEM WAS SORRY he'd come to. It was less painful to be unconscious. The top of his head stung like a motherfucker. A throbbing sting that grew in intensity. Just when he thought he could bear it, the pain got worse.

The whiskey he was swallowing would have tasted a whole lot better without all the blood in his mouth. Even still, it helped with the pain.

James was asking him all kinds of fool questions about Bill's outburst. Something about James just didn't sit right. Clem had been aware of this for a while. It was the money that tipped him off. James had fought like hell to stop Bart taking the silver dollars off him, but then he'd handed them over meekly when Clem and the others got the drop on him. It was almost as if he didn't think the money belonged to him. Clem had come to suspect he should have listened to Bart before he let James in.

None of that mattered now though. Clem was going to die soon. If not from the scalping, then from the monstrous hair that was tearing down the town. James was the closest thing he had to a confessor.

"This is a sacred place to the Navajos. A secret they

kept for centuries. In fact most of *them* don't even know about it. We only learned about it by accident. We were on the run from the law at the time."

"We?" said James. "Would that mean you and Bill?"

"And the other members of the Baldwin Gang. Named after Bill, that's his name, William Baldwin. Wasn't Bill put the gang together, that was Edward Davies. Bill took over after Edward got his fool head blown off, second time we robbed a train. We did pretty good for a while. Made a lot of money and spread a lot of money around. That way no one went blabbing to the law and we always had a place to hide.

"Problem started when we robbed a train with federal wages. Thought we'd hit the jackpot at first. Then we discovered we'd stolen a military pay roll. They weren't gonna rest until every member of the gang was swinging from a scaffold. Right alongside everyone who ever helped us. Soon ran out of places to hide after that.

"We split up to avoid detection and they picked us off, one by one. Me and Bill ended up hiding out in the wilds, living off whatever we could kill and nearly starving as a result. We was stalking this hare when we saw this young injun shoot and make off with it. We followed him, meaning to kill him and take back the hare.

"He lead us to this hidden plateau, where this ol' injun was waiting for him. We thought we'd wait while they skinned and cooked the hare for us, then we'd kill 'em. But instead of cooking the hare they performed this weird ceremony and opened up a sort of shimmering gateway in thin air. We couldn't believe what we was seeing. It didn't make any sense, it was almost as if we couldn't look at it without losing a part of our minds. You probably had the same feeling when *you* saw it.

"Then we saw the ol' injun passing stuff back and forth with other injuns who lived inside the gateway. Eventually the shimmering gateway started to get smaller and then it just disappeared. After that they cleared everything away and burned the hare. While they was doing that, we lay in wait and ambushed 'em as they left.

"We beat up on 'em a little, to get 'em to tell us what they was doing, but they refused. They was only an old man and a young boy, but they stood up to some rough treatment. Finally we roasted the old injun's feet over a fire till he gave in.

"The old bastard told us he was opening a portal to a magical realm that existed outside of time and space. He called it the Eternal Dreaming. It was part of the place that our souls go to when we dream. It had been cultivated by the Navajos like the maize that they grew. They'd coaxed it into being a tiny bit at a time, building a living space out of tiny bits of dream, knitted together over generations till they had a whole realm. That's why nothing grows here, it's not part of the normal world."

"What about hair, that grows here."

"The Navajos believe that a man's hair is the physical manifestation of his dreams. That's what the ol' injun told us. I remember an injun scout we had back in the war, refused to cut his hair because he'd lose his edge if he did. Said it sharpened his intuition. It was his dreams you see, spilling out of his scalp, day by day. In a land made up of dreams, hair's the only thing that's gonna grow."

"Maybe, I dunno."

"You don't know shit. You wanna hear this story or not?"

"Okay, calm down."

"So this Eternal Dreaming is a place where their ancestors live for all eternity. Only the wisest and most pure of their medicine men and women were chosen to live there. They would pass over before they died and stay there forever more, without ever aging, getting sick or dying. The ol' injun's family had been tending to the needs of the ancestors for countless generations. His bloodline was part of the magic that anchored the place to this world. The care and tending of the Eternal Dreaming was passed on from parent to child throughout the ages.

"Course, soon as we heard about this place, where you never got old and died, where the law couldn't touch you, we knew we had to get in there. So we tortured them both till they opened the portal for us. Then we put a knife to their throats and threatened to kill the boy and the ol' injun if the ancestors didn't let us pass through the portal.

"They tried to warn us off, telling us that once we stepped through we could never leave, but we didn't pay no heed to that. See, they knew that if the boy and the ol' injun died, then they'd lose their anchor to this world, so they had to let us in.

"I held a knife to the ol' injun's neck while Big Bill jumped through the weird shimmering hole between this place and the outside. Then he threatened to scalp the head ancestor, an old Navajo called Tsiishch'ili, if they didn't let me in. I jumped over as it was closing up. Nearly didn't get my foot through in time. Got a helluva shock, just like you did.

"Once we were inside we took a look around and decided the place was a goldmine waiting to happen. It was the perfect hideout. We could charge huge amounts of money to outlaws who wanted to avoid the law and live forever. We could even run rackets on the outside without fear of getting caught. All we had to do was tidy the place up a bit, make it fit for proper white folks, and get rid of the injuns that were living there.

"They'd avoided us ever since we arrived. Being all mystic and such, they weren't violent like us, and they were much older. We knew they were plotting to get rid of us, so we struck before they got a chance to do anything.

"We rounded 'em all up and told 'em we were taking over. Then we forced 'em to tell us how the place worked and what we needed to do to control it. We tied 'em all up and started torturing 'em. We scalped the first couple we went to work on. Thing was, they almost seemed relieved that we took their whole scalps off and not just their hair. They seemed terrified of cutting their hair.

"So the next thing we did was shave a couple of their heads. That's when we found out about the ingrowing. It's also how we learned what to do with the things you become if you cut your hair. The injuns told us how to use the swamp bark to knock out and kill one of 'em. Didn't have to torture 'em none to get that information neither.

"After that, they just gave up and told us everything we wanted to know. We got them to perform a ceremony that put is in control of the whole place. They assured us that it would belong to me and Bill, but mostly Bill, for all eternity. Or, as they put it, for as long as the sun shines, the grass grows and the rivers flow. That's what Bill was talking about when he said he'd had assurances.

"They also performed a rite putting the ol' injun and the young brave in our power, so they would serve us and keep the Eternal Dreaming intact for as long as their bloodline existed. The ol'injun died but the young brave grew up to be that wily bastard Rivers Flow. We corrupted him over time, and he got to like the power and the money Dead Scalp brought him. Dead Scalp was what we renamed the place.

"Course Rivers Flow got too greedy in the end and that's what undid him. Maybe it was that young Mexican spitfire he took in, I hear she developed rich tastes. Anyway, he tried to rip off Bill and that cost him his two young sons. He started muttering about getting even with Bill for a while, but he soon forgot about that."

Clem drained the last of the whiskey. It hit the back of his throat and he breathed it in. Great wracking coughs burst from his chest as his body tried to get the whiskey out of his lungs. Each hack and splutter set off explosions inside his cranium. Stars burst behind the eyelids he'd squeezed tight.

Clem kept his eyelids shut as the searing, harrowing pain took over his head. Murdered every thought inside it and took hold of all his senses. Clem realized there wasn't much point holding on to life, if this was all he had to look forward to. Death was better than this torture and disfigurement.

He'd lost his taste for life anyway. The monotony and the drudge of life in Dead Scalp had worn him down. Nothing ever changed. Everything lost its flavor. The joy and the thrill of life were slowly sucked out of a man. Even gambling and sex had become pointless. He may as well be dead. At least this way he'd cheat the blasted hair.

He travelled through the red mist of pain into an endless, numb blackness. Like the Eternal Dreaming, Clem knew that this was a place from which he'd never return.

This realization brought him more relief than he'd ever known in his entire life.

CHAPTER 1 0

J AMES WATCHED AS Clem quit coughing, dropped the bottle and stopped breathing altogether. He hoped Bill wouldn't blame him for Clem's death.

He stood and peered out from behind the closed shutters. Nothing moved on the central street except for the hair that was growing up the sides of the buildings, including the saloon. James and Bill could very well be the last two people alive.

Bill burst back in through the connecting door. His arms were full of carved stones, a couple of weird looking rattles and a brazier. Bill dumped all this on his desk and glanced over at Clem. "'S'matter with him?" he said.

"He died," said James. "I'm sorry, I know he was your friend."

Bill was quiet for a moment and stared hard at the floor. He seemed to be choking back his grief, so as not to show any type of weakness in front of another man. James was cautious enough not to say a word while Bill was like this. Finally, he nodded and seemed to come back to himself.

Bill swept all the papers and other objects from his

desk. "Gimme a hand with this," he said, arranging the brazier and other objects in a careful pattern. Before James could do anything, both windows exploded inwards and the shutters were torn from their hinges.

James wheeled round to see a tide of hair pouring through the windows and over the floor. James lunged for one of the sabers. Bill scrabbled with some matches and swamp bark.

James slashed at the hair which moved out of his way, then wrapped itself around both his wrists. He was yanked off his feet and pulled back towards the wall, where the hair pinned him with his hands above his head. Bill had also been pinned to the wall with his hands over his head before he could light any bark.

More and more hair pushed its way into the room. The loose strands began to interweave themselves, creating complex plaits. The plaits formed themselves into two columns that looked like legs and feet. Then the legs continued to grow upwards, weaving a torso and then a head and two arms complete with hands.

The figure that now stood before them looked like a wise, elderly injun woven entirely from hair. The figure crossed its arms and stared implacably at Big Bill.

Bill narrowed his eyes and smiled a cold humorless smile. James could see he recognized the figure that stood before them.

"Tsiishch'ili, you redskin, sumbitch," he said. "What in hell do you think you're doing here?"

"William Baldwin," said the figure, in a voice that sounded like a thousand knotted strands of hair being brushed apart. "Weren't you just about to summon me?"

"Only to kick your red ass back down to whatever hell I sent it to in the first place!"

"It would seem to me, that I'm not the one who is currently in hell."

"Is that why you're doing this? Trying to destroy my town. You want to send us all to hell, huh?"

"I'm not the one who's responsible for this."

"Oh really? Well, forgive me for asking just who the fuck *is* responsible, if it's not you? See, this hair comes for the graveyard where we stuck your corpse. So it's already got your stink all over it."

"Are you still so ignorant of what's really happening? Have you not known all along why only hair grows here? This is a part of the dreaming world. The hair is your dreams made manifest. It is simply your worst nightmares given substance. Your subconscious fears of retribution finally surfacing. I'm not even Tsiishch'ili, just a guilty memory that still lurks in your subconscious."

"Don't try and wriggle out of this. You swore to me, when you did the ceremony and handed this place over. It would all belong to me as long as the sun shines, the grass grows and the rivers flow!"

"This is a land outside of time and space. No rivers flow here and no grass grows either, that's not even the sun shining in the sky. While we're talking of swearing, do you not recall that you swore you would let us all live? But the moment the ceremony was over you butchered me and my fellow shamans."

"We did what we had to. I ain't about to apologize. We brought some order to this place. We brought trade and we brought commerce. We found all kinds of ways to exploit what you were wasting and we got rich off the back of it. It don't belong to you savages anymore. This is American territory. You can't have it back no matter how much hair you send."

"As I said, William Baldwin, this is not hair. These are your dreams, breaking through the soil. This is your American dream, rising up to choke you, as you always knew it would."

"We had a deal!"

"Which you broke when you severed the blood line and killed Rivers Flow's children."

"We didn't sever shit. That old Redskin can have more brats any time. We might have killed his kids but we didn't kill Rivers Flow and that's what counts. The bloodline is still intact. We're still anchored to the outside world. The deal still stands. You can't be here. Now get the hell out of my town before I choke you with your own guts all over again."

"Ah yes, I'm very glad you mentioned that. It makes this so much more poetic."

The figure of Tsiishch'ili unfolded his arms and pointed at Bill. His arm unravelled itself and the loose strands shot towards Bill's face. Bill struggled, tossing his head backwards and forwards, but the hairs forced his jaws apart and a whole trunk of them plunged down his throat.

Blood trickled from the corner of Bill's mouth. His legs went into spasms and he beat his palms against the wall, cracking the wood. His head bent backwards and the hair began to withdraw.

Bill grabbed instinctively at the trunk of hair, but he couldn't stop it as it left his throat and tore his intestines out of his mouth. Blood dripped down Bill's chin as his lower colon was yanked from between his dislocated jaws.

James saw Bill blink with disbelief, as the hair wrapped his intestines around his neck and pulled them tight. Bill's face went from red to purple. It swelled up with the pressure and his eyeballs bulged so much in their sockets, that James was afraid they would pop out of his head.

James could hardly believe that Bill was still alive, let alone filled with righteous indignation that the injuns had dared to cross him. He went to his death believing that Dead Scalp still belonged to him according to the terms of the agreement.

James knew that wasn't the case though. He also knew now why the old devil he'd got the silver dollars from, was so easy to rob.

Everyone had said it couldn't be done, that the place had too many men and was too well guarded, but James was desperate and up against it. He needed the ten thousand entry fee so bad, he was prepared to rob Dead Scalp itself. To make off with the money they kept on the outside, under Rivers Flow's watchful eye. It seemed kind of fitting to use Dead Scalp's own money to buy his way into the place. So long as they didn't find out, he'd have nothing to worry about.

Rivers Flow had put up no fight as James filled his saddle bags. Then he'd accompanied him to the plateau and performed the ceremony to open the portal, just like James told him.

At the last minute, just as the portal was about to open, Rivers Flow had grabbed the saddle bags and made a dash for it. James had chased him behind a big boulder nearby. He was much older than James and couldn't run as fast.

James had knocked him to the ground, but Rivers

Flow wouldn't give up the saddlebags. So James had taken the knife from his boot and plunged it into the old devil's heart.

James had been wiping the blood off his knife as the portal opened. James hadn't been too bothered about this, with Rivers Flow gone there were no loose ends. What bothered him though, was why Rivers Flow had smiled as James pushed the knife between his ribs. Why he seemed so satisfied.

As the hair closed in on him James knew at last. When he killed Rivers Flow, James had severed the bloodline and sentenced everyone in Dead Scalp to death, before he'd even entered. Rivers Flow had smiled because he'd finally got his revenge on Big Bill for the murder of his sons.

The hair swarmed over James like a final revelation. He knew that no sun would shine, no grass would grow and no rivers would flow for anyone in Dead Scalp ever again.

AFTERWORD

JOHN LLEWELLYN PROBERT

Did you enjoy that? Or were you—quite rightly I should think—shocked, horrified and possibly even a little offended by some of what Mr Jasper Bark has offered to you over the preceding pages? I know I was, and so it has fallen to me to give you some inkling of the kind of fate that befalls such authors who dare to produce such outrageously entertaining fiction.

Where did Jasper Bark come from? I honestly don't know. But if the stories in this collection are anything to go by, I can guess where he might be going:

The scene is a courtroom. Not a nice, brightly-lit, American-style courtroom—the kind you see on television shows that have comfy seats, intimidating but essentially kindly judges played by African American actors who have made a career out of this sort of thing, and lady lawyers with big hair played by actresses who are just ever-so-slightly past their prime and very behind on their payments for their excessive and inappropriate visits to the tanning salon.

Oh no.

This is a proper, old-fashioned, British courtroom.

Poorly lit and panelled in dusty, scabrous oak that is weary from absorbing the pitiful cries of those who have been accused within these walls and, more importantly, sentenced to ensure that they will never commit such sordid atrocities again.

The immense and ancient judge has sat in his sagging leather chair for such a long time that he has become one with it, his cynical world-weary flesh having fused with the dead animal skin with which it has stayed in contact for so long. He knows he can never leave this place. He knows he will die here, and the inevitability of his slow decay has only made his attitude to those brought before him all the more merciless.

One is to be brought before him today.

An author.

An author of horror stories.

To look at him, though, you might not think him to be the kind of person to have created the horrific works of so-called art of which he stands accused.

No, not stands. A swift blow to the left loin by one of the brutish, near Neanderthal guards who have dragged him into the courtroom soon puts paid to that.

Now he kneels accused. Gasps accused.

Crawls accused.

The judge leans forward as far as his attachments of leathery skin will allow. When he speaks his voice resembles a worn-out foghorn on a windy night.

"Do you feel ashamed?"

The author takes a moment to gather his breath and wipe the trickle of blood that has seeped from the corner of his mouth. He is about to say something when another sharp blow, this time to the back of his neck, prevents it.

"And so you should," the judge continues, picking up a dirty, bloodstained manuscript and peering with rheumy, jaundiced sclerae at the first page.

"Stuck. On. You." Each word sounds like a statement. Of fact. Of guilt.

Of deserving damnation.

"You wrote this?"

The author again draws breath to speak, then thinks better of it and nods instead.

"Vile." The judge flicks through the pages until he comes to another story. "Unspeakably vile. Feeding a decent, law-abiding citizen their own brains? Bricking someone up to be bathed in the filth of others? A mad girl who dresses up as a nurse and tries to kill her own child?" His eyes blaze. "Mocking the very devil himself? If I were a younger man I would insist your face be rubbed in the contents of the bowels you have thought it so amusing to construct a map of the London Underground out of."

The author says nothing. He knows he is guilty of what this court perceives as his 'crimes'. All that remains is for him to be sentenced.

Rough hands drag him to the place that has been reserved for him, the place that has always been there, waiting for just the right kind of person to occupy it.

The author is forced into the chair. The teak of its frame, awakening quickly to the presence of its longed-for occupant, grows around him and into him, imprisoning him forever, making him as much a part of these proceedings as the others here. Powerless to resist, he can do nothing as his fingers reach of their own accord for the typewriter keys, and become melded to them.

"We've always needed a stenographer," the judge rasps as wires burst from the typewriter casing and drill into the author's skull, fixing his gaze on the yellowing sheet of paper that has appeared in the typewriter's carriage. "You should do nicely."

So please remember, ladies and gentlemen, should you ever feel the urge to read these tales a second time. Jasper Bark suffered to bring these stories to you. In fact he's probably still suffering now if there's any justice. And I don't doubt some of those court cases he records may find their way into future collections, if their publishers don't know what's good for them. I just ask you to spare the poor man a thought as he types away, eyes and fingers welded in place for his own good. Forever.

ACKNOWLEDGEMENTS

I hate acknowledgements in books. I usually skip over them if they're at the front or ignore them if they're at the back. This is why I hardly notice, until years later, when other writers are kind enough to acknowledge me.

Acknowledgements always sound like a protracted Oscar acceptance to me. I can't help but picture the author in a big glittery tiara, with mascara streaked tears pooling in his beard, as he sobs his way through a thousand heartfelt thanks to everyone from his nursery teacher to his agent.

Long acknowledgements have the feel of a lap of honour. As an author myself, I know what a sweet victory it is every time your name appears on a new book. And you have to understand how we authors love to bask in the glow of something that's only been accomplished by over a million people before us. Even still, all that back patting just makes me a bit nauseous.

However, I do owe a lot of people for their help and contributions to this collection, and there's only so far blackmail and extortion will go before you have to start saying thank you.

My editor and friend Joe Mynhardt and his wife Annemie were great to me and my family when we visited them in South Africa and took us out for a lovely meal. What's more, Joe has been a fantastic editor to work with and has provided huge support for my work, and one day I will burn those negatives, I promise.

Rob Moran, is a man whose moroseness and constant misanthropy never fail to bring joy and laughter into my life. As jaw-droppingly talented artists go, I don't think I could have gotten stuck with a better one.

I've loved Pat Cadigan's writing for years. It was a huge honour to read alongside her and to draw her into the Bloodfudge prank. She provided an intro that was far superior to anything I could have hoped for.

I met John Llewellyn Probert in the not so funny pages when our stories appeared alongside one another. John has since become a highly valued collaborator and co-conspirator. He and his wife Kate, who writes as the talented Thana Niveau, have also become great friends. Didn't he write a glorious afterword?

Lisa Jenkins, a gifted writer and editor, went above and beyond in helping me get the text of 'Stuck On You' into a proper shape. You are a star.

Emma Audsley is a talented writer and dedicated editor who runs the Horrifically Horrifying Horror Blog and Screaming Skull Press. Her eagle eye kept the collection free of so many typos.

The stories in this collection might not have been written had it not been for commissions from a whole host of wonderful editors including Jonathan Oliver, Ross Warren, Suzy Goodall, Michael Wilson, Adele Wearing, Theresa Derwin, Jo Thomas, and Margrét Helgadóttir.

I also have to thank Jim Mcleod, Ann Giardina Magee, Tim Cundle, Jim Dodge, Dianne Hunt, Joe Gordon, Kevin Lintner, Matthew Tait, Matthew Fryer, Cory Cline, Colum McKnight, Andrew Angel, Vix Kirkpatrick, Matthew Scott Baker, Blaze McRobb, Joan De La Haye, Jim Goforth, Armand Rosamilia, Promote Horror, Simon Marshall-Jones, Adele Cosgrove-Bray, and the Indie Horror Blog for supporting me and my work in the blogosphere.

I should also thank my very eloquent friend and fellow author Joseph D'Lacey because he thanked me in one of his books several years ago and I only just read it last week. Told you I never read these pages.

CONNECT WITH JASPER BARK

Website:
http://www.jasperbark.com/
Facebook:
https://www.facebook.com/jaspre.bark
Twitter:
https://twitter.com/jasperbark
@jasperbark

Connect with Crystal Lake Publishing

Website (be sure to sign up for our newsletter):
www.crystallakepub.com
Facebook:
www.facebook.com/Crystallakepublishing
Twitter:
https://twitter.com/crystallakepub

We hope you enjoyed this title. If so, we would be grateful if you could leave a review on your blog or one of the many websites open to book reviews. Reviews are essential for a successful book. And remember to keep an eye out for more of our books. We have collections by Daniel I. Russell, Kevin Lucia, William Meikle and Gary McMahon, as well as novellas and anthologies.

THANK YOU FOR PURCHASING THIS BOOK